Oyster

MARIANNE ACKERMAN

Oyster

a novel

DUNDURN PRESS

Publisher and acquiring editor: Meghan Macdonald | Editor: Robyn So
Cover designer: Karen Alexiou
Cover image: Wachiraphorn / istock.com

Library and Archives Canada Cataloguing in Publication

Title: Oyster : a novel / Marianne Ackerman.
Names: Ackerman, Marianne, author.
Identifiers: Canadiana (print) 20250306603 | Canadiana (ebook) 20250309947 | ISBN 9781459757059 (softcover) | ISBN 9781459757042 (PDF) | ISBN 9781459757035 (EPUB)
Subjects: LCGFT: Novels.
Classification: LCC PS8551.C33 O97 2026 | DDC C813/.54—dc23

We acknowledge the support of the Canada Council for the Arts and the Ontario Arts Council for our publishing program. We also acknowledge the financial support of the Government of Ontario, through the Ontario Book Publishing Tax Credit and Ontario Creates, and the Government of Canada.

Printed and bound in Canada.

Dundurn Press
1382 Queen Street East
Toronto, Ontario, Canada M4L 1C9
dundurn.com, @dundurnpress

To my father, for the many great stories he told.
Ralph Leo Ackerman, 1926–2007

PART I

Fall

1

Sunday morning, the middle of a heat wave. I was lying in a cold bath when the phone rang. Normally, I wouldn't bother getting out but the ring had a sense of urgency. It was Dan, his voice so calm it sounded false: Dad's hurt. He fell off the roof.

I got dressed, stuffed an overnight bag with essentials, and headed out to the car. Turning onto the Don Valley, I remembered the newspaper. Without a vacation stop it would pile up and signal nobody's home. Had I even locked the door? Too late to go back. I fished a pen out of my purse and scribbled a note on my hand.

On a good day, the drive from Cabbagetown to Prince Edward County takes just over two hours. I usually stop midway for coffee and a few honey cruller Timbits, counting on a blast of sugar and caffeine to keep alert, but I was frantic to reach the farm. My mind was racing. How could an eighty-two-year-old man fall off the roof of a three-storey house? More to the point, what was he doing on the roof? How did he even get up there? Beethoven's *Pastoral* came on the car radio, a beautiful rolling symphony. I cranked up the volume, opened the windows. I had to lean in, grip the steering wheel just to keep my eyes focused. In the forefront of my mind crowding out all else was the image of a tiny grey-haired man, arms spread wide, floating to the ground like a feather. Surely, he would have landed on a bush. He's in a coma. He'll wake up and give us a perfectly good explanation.

The exit sign popped up out of nowhere. One foot barely touched the brake, but a transport had been edging up behind and bumped the fender, sending my little Morris Cooper into a gravel spin. I closed my eyes, held on tight as we flew into the air and landed with a thud. The music stopped.

My first thought was the gas tank's going to explode. The door handle was stuck. I slid over to the passenger seat, climbed through the window and ran, stumbling into a field of wildflowers. Queen Anne's lace, black-eyed Susans, goldenrod, blue devil. An unnatural quiet bore down, broken only by the faint buzz of bees. My head was throbbing. For a moment I thought I'd gone deaf. The heat was intense. I reached down to pick a daisy, noticed red drops. Touched my burning lip, triggering a gush of blood. The sky dipped, turned dark.

The next thing I knew, two muscular medics were lifting me onto a stretcher. A young policewoman was holding my hand, telling me to stay awake. I tried to say, Call Dan or Edie, they live in the County. The number's in my wallet, but my tongue was swollen, I could hardly get the words out. She said, Don't worry, he's on his way. Such lovely blue eyes, thick dark hair pulled off her face, a sweet mouth. What would draw a girl like that to the awkward cut of a police uniform? I wanted to ask, but she kept talking.

You're the writer Amelia Cameron, aren't you? Sorry, I had to look in your purse for ID. I really enjoyed your novel. We took it in English lit. You know, it's one of the few books I hang onto. Too bad I don't have it here. I'd like to get your autograph.

Mercifully, her phone rang and she wandered off to take the call.

Strapped into a horizontal position on the gurney, neck held firmly in a brace, I had nothing to do but stare up at the sky and watch cumulus clouds float by. *Erosion*. Lord, that was decades ago, her age when I wrote it. Five novels since, another in the works. Only as they lifted the stretcher into an ambulance did I catch a glimpse of the scene. Police cars, fire trucks, stranded motorists milling around behind a fence of yellow tape. The transport, beached like a comatose whale, blocked the highway. Traffic backed up to the horizon. An awful wave of dread. What if people were badly hurt or dead? I dearly hoped not, for their sake, and for Harold's. At a time like this, he surely deserved our undivided attention.

Dan pulled into the parking lot just as the ambulance was about to drive off. He insisted on riding with me while one of the junior police officers followed with his Mercedes. My elder brother by a year, Dan Cameron has a knack for getting people to step in line, do what he wants. Handed the task of keeping me awake, he embraced the opportunity to lecture: Thousands of dollars of damage back there. Thank God nobody's hurt, or worse. That's all I can say. Could have been a tragedy.

No, Dan. A tragedy is a dramatic or prose work of —

Don't make light of things, Milly. Not at a time like this.

I assured him I wasn't making light, I was in pain. Every bone in my body ached. Might even have whiplash. And what about Mini? Was my poor little car badly damaged?

Total write-off.

How he enjoyed announcing the news.

Dan's network of contacts extended to the hospital in Picton. I was seen by a doctor right away, poked, x-rayed, tested, and sent off with a prescription for pain pills and instructions on how to treat a swollen lip. Only when we were safely locked into the air-conditioned comfort of his beloved Merc did I register the full meaning of my trip to the County.

He's dead, isn't he?

Yes, he is. Buckle up your seatbelt.

Why didn't you tell me on the phone?

I was afraid you'd be hysterical and crash your car.

He bristled when I said I'd have to see the body before I'd believe Harold was really gone. On his eightieth birthday, I had resolved to think of our father as a person, to refer to him by the name he was given at birth, out of respect. He was a shadowy figure when we were growing up, more often quoted by our mother than heard from in person. My late-life interest in Harold Cameron, the man, irritated my brother immensely.

We hardly spoke on the way to the farm. I pretended to sleep, but as we turned into the lane leading up to the house, I caught Dan's attention drift to his vineyard, ten acres of Merlot lovingly tended on a south-facing part of the farm. Harold had railed against the venture, calling it the Devil's Vineyard, a city slicker's folly that was doomed to end in bankruptcy. He took great delight in ridiculing the enterprise, a natural reaction, I suppose, to the hostile attitude Dan had taken to farming since he was old enough to do chores. Or, maybe he'd secretly enjoyed watching his cocky eldest son come around to the land in middle age, if only by way of a hobby. In the hours after his death every thought of my father gave rise to questions.

Edie was waiting at the kitchen door to welcome me with hugs and tears. The only demonstrative member of the family, my sister-in-law has a knack for slicing through the cone of silence that descends on any untypical situation affecting born-and-bred County Camerons. When Dan disappeared into the parlour to take a call from the funeral home, she filled me in on what few details they had: A woman living in the bungalow down the road had found him. He'd gone up on the roof in the middle of a windstorm to adjust the satellite dish and ended up a twisted figure, sprawled out on the lawn. Whether he was dead on impact or died on the way to the hospital, nobody seemed to know. The police were investigating. We'd just have to wait.

I went upstairs to freshen up. One look in the bathroom mirror revealed the reason for Edie's distress. A thick dark circle had formed around my eye. My cheek bulged, pushing the eyebrow into an upside-down V over the bruise. The other side sagged, as if it had let go with the jolt of landing. I am ashamed to say the first tears I shed after my father's death were brought on by the sight of my battered face, and by thoughts of greeting people I hadn't seen in years at the funeral home visitations.

My sister-in-law is a wonderful homemaker. She places great importance on the restorative power of food, so although I wasn't the least bit hungry, refusing dinner was out of the question. While we ate, Dan laid out the funeral plans and travel status of our two siblings. Lance had booked a flight from Vancouver. Jean was out of touch in Africa, no other way to tell her than by blunt email. She'd answered immediately, said she was looking into flights and would let us know. I asked if anybody had thought to call Calgary, inform Jean's ex or their daughter, Ginny. Dan had assumed Jean would convey the news. Don't count on it, I said. In the decade since Jean and Ravi's divorce, I'd had very little contact with my sister or her family. Edie offered to get in touch. She urged me to spend the night at their house, but I declined, saying I needed to sleep in my old room at a time like this.

As soon as they left, I regretted not taking up her offer. I wandered around in a daze, thoroughly winded yet wide awake, feet still not touching the ground. As far back as any of us could remember the Camerons had died discreetly of ordinary causes. Harold broke the mould. He was fit as a fiddle. On a windy Saturday night, he went up on the roof of the house he'd grown up in and fell to his death. A neighbour found him and called 911. That's all we had to go on.

Walking into the parlour, knowing my father would not be sitting in his striped smoker perusing the *Picton Gazette* was a strange experience. The atmosphere seemed charged, as if he had just that minute stepped out of sight. I was sure I could smell the sweet aroma of his pipe. The room was familiar but at the same time unreal, like a stage set for an old-fashioned murder mystery: grey- and cream-striped wallpaper, ridiculously high ceilings marked with water stains and cracks in the plaster, a sagging sofa last upholstered years ago in rose velvet with matching drapes, just before our mother became sick. It had once looked stately next to the dark mahogany china cabinet and buffet. The room seemed to vibrate, as if wracked by a death rattle, one last sigh before collapsing into oblivion. *We're orphans now*, I thought. Old orphans. I found a bottle of Canadian Club in the cabinet, poured a generous shot, and sat down in Harold's smoker to wait for the news to settle in.

2

Virginia Gupta missed the red-eye out of Calgary but managed to catch a later flight. She hired a limo at the airport, didn't want to bother us. There was a massive traffic snarl on the 401, then the driver, who'd never had a fare east of Toronto, overshot the exit, tried to circle back, and got lost. A litany of travails conveyed in frantic texts, her journey kept a full house of mourners waiting forty-two minutes.

As she entered the church, the organist set into "Amazing Grace" and the mourners stood. All heads turned her way. She was dressed completely in white: billowy, skirt-like pants and a loose-fitting blouse. Her waist-length black hair flowing as she strode up the aisle like a celebrity, she slid into the pew in front of me beside her cousin Frank, who had saved her a seat. She seemed to curl up, make herself small, as if the grand entrance had been too much attention. He took her hand, and I thought, *She's still the same dear Ginny, brash yet needy, a bundle of contradictions.*

After too many years without contact with my cherished niece, I was overjoyed to see her, even if it took a funeral to bring us together. I had to bite down hard on the inside of my cheek to keep from crying. Edie gave me a nudge, whispered, She wants to be a writer, like you. She's moving east in September. At that exact moment Ginny turned around and smiled at me. Big brown eyes made bold by liner, flashy lips, sparkly cheeks beaming, a look that said, isn't that exciting? I smiled back. A writer, that is interesting.

With the exception of Ginny, whose father hails from a vast Hindu family rooted in the Indian province of Goa, the Cameron clan of Prince Edward County is white-bread Canadian. United Empire Loyalist stock on the Cameron side, Irish Catholic on our mother's. Harold had scandalized his people by converting to marry Madeline Callaghan, which is why we gathered at St. Gregory's for his funeral, because we are Catholic to the core, even if some strains of the Celtic spirit did not survive the fusion. We're County-bred. We don't go in for professional criers, like the Greeks, to express our feelings. The ritual set in motion by death is designed to ensure that no one has time or space to unravel. In the case of a patriarch who died suddenly, accidentally, at eighty-two, surviving kin, mature offspring, and nearly grown-up grandchildren are expected to show up well-dressed and serve as a quiet backdrop to the main event.

Dan took the podium, the crowd settled back. As far as I knew, my elder brother was most comfortable in jeans and T-shirt, sometimes a hard hat, although he hadn't done much manual labour in ages. He drove a shiny black SUV with his company logo on the door, doled out assurance to clients who, over the years, had made him wealthy. Edie managed the household. A cheerleader when they met and ten years younger than Dan, she has excellent taste. He was wearing a trim, dark suit, quite slimming, with a cream shirt and paisley tie. He carried a roll of paper, typed by his secretary. I'd seen him rehearsing in the backyard, chopping the air for effect, stopping to scratch out or add a phrase. When I asked if he needed an audience, he said no thanks, it is what it is, and walked away.

Short on biographical details, Dan's eulogy was ardent, civic-minded, I would even say inspiring. I hardly recognized the man he spoke about. Who knew Harold Cameron was so interested in community building and resource management? He'd never mentioned any of this in my presence. When Dan finished, the crowd broke into applause, an emphatically secular response confirming my suspicion that many of those present were Dan's professional contacts. Showing up, being part of the give-and-take between important persons, applause was not inappropriate. It relieved the tension. Father John thanked Dan warmly and asked if anyone wanted to add a few words.

I don't know what came over me. I jumped up and was staring at a forehead-high microphone before I remembered how terrifying it is to speak in front of people. Everyone was looking straight at me, at the ugly bruise of my left eye, which I'd tried and failed to cover with makeup and thought about constantly. Seconds inched by. When I started to speak, a piercing, shudder-inducing whine came out of the sound system. An altar girl stepped forward to adjust the mic. I mumbled something about missing Dad. Blinded by fright, I did not notice Frank making his way to the front until he was standing at my side. I stumbled back to the seat, throbbing with embarrassment, and sank into the pew, convinced the thunder of my heartbeat could be heard by all.

The eldest of three boys, Frank is his father's nemesis. From the time he was old enough to express an opinion, they've disagreed on just about everything. It soon became evident that he had inherited one of Dan's most effective qualities, the knack for holding a room. He spoke without notes, thanked me for expressing so eloquently what we're all feeling, for adding a touch of humanity to the proceedings. Then he began to talk about his grandfather, recounting experiences they'd shared. How Grandpa had taught him to drive — on the tractor. Given him his first beer. Told him everything he needed to know about girls: Love them well, and they will love you back. He talked about Dad's attitude to money: take care of pennies, forget about the bank account. His habit of losing at euchre: He always blamed the cards. Frank's warmth and detailed observation brought the departed back to life, left the assembled laughing and wiping away tears. At just the right moment, his tone shifted. He said he and his grandfather had talked a lot about death during the past few months: Grandpa was old, he knew it, and he wasn't afraid. He swore he'd go out in some spectacular way. And he did, didn't he? He told me he left instructions for the kind of send-off he should be given. He wanted to be cremated and have his ashes scattered somewhere on the farm, preferably not in the barnyard. Otherwise, our choice. I saw that letter, don't know what happened to it, but the send-off he talked about, well, it wasn't this. Maybe he changed his mind. Old people do. But if you ask me — okay, here's the thing — I'm going by the instructions Grandpa gave *me*, which I passed on to the bros — Glenn and Tom — and to Cousin Ginny, his descendants. He said he didn't want a solemn occasion. He wanted a party with good friends and family present. So I'm inviting everybody back to his house, where you'll be entertained with a band we've put together especially for the occasion. Glenn is ready to hit the beer store. Give us a show of hands if you can make it. Tom'll be waiting outside with a hat. Drop him a fiver on the way out of the building, er, church. We'll meet you back at the farm with a truckload of brewskies. Oh, hey, if you want to go home and change into something you're not afraid to puke on, please do so. Come on, who's with us?

Hands shot up. I could not resist seeking out a glimpse of Dan. His jaw was rigid. Absolutely nothing to be done.

As the church emptied, Lance donned a flashy pair of sunglasses and made his way straight to Ginny and Frank, who were absorbed in the after-party plans. Dressed in a pale blue seersucker jacket and white pants, he was an easy fit with their youthful exuberance, until Dan stomped over and hauled him back to his duty as one of the adult mourners.

Edie and I got into the back seat of the funeral limo. Dan sat in the front. Lance squeezed in between us and immediately launched into the question of Harold's funeral instructions, as recounted by Frank. We'll talk later, Dan growled, and told the driver to move. We rode in silence to the cemetery, where Father John said farewell prayers and tossed a handful of clay onto the box. Dan made a sonorous interjection on behalf of our absent sister, Jean, who, he said, had sincerely wanted to be present but couldn't leave the orphanage in Rwanda when a new well was being drilled. Dad would understand, he said. He'd always been a great believer in the importance of good drinking water. The corpse of our father was lowered into the ground, encased in a coffin worth as much as a good used tractor.

3

The Cameron homestead is perched on a hill amid two hundred acres of mostly fertile farmland. The acreage and a modest, earlier version of the frame house were purchased by Alford Cameron in the mid-1800s. His grandfather Emerald had fled north during the American Revolution out of loyalty to the British, but we've always considered Alford to be the founder of our family. He was the first to live in the age of photography, which may account for his immortality. His sepia studio portrait suggests a fierce temperament encased in a small, compact body. He is seated, his wife, Alice, standing beside him, a tall, stout lady bundled in dark taffeta, exuding strength and resolve.

Built by Alford, who clearly had money if not great architectural vision, the house has twelve large rooms, impressive but impossible to heat, especially the second floor, and all the showy features of Victorian times, a mansard roof and wraparound porch with elaborate ornamental trim. Oak and maple trees were planted around the whole grand structure in the 1960s, and over the years grew to just about hide a cluster of decaying barns and sheds stretching out behind. From south-facing bay windows in the parlour, the blue-grey expanse of Lake Ontario is barely visible in the distance.

Every summer since Mom died, Harold undertook to mow further into the sloping pasture, until the front lawn came to resemble a golf course. Dan gave him an expensive ride-on mower for his seventieth birthday, which sped up the conquest. As far as I know, he never set foot on the acres of grass, though he loved to sit on the front porch with a cup of instant coffee and gaze at it. My comments on the environmental impact of incessant mowing went in one ear and out the other. I can only imagine that after a lifetime of hard labour, market-gardening, raising beef cattle and chickens, Harold took pleasure from this relatively painless — if pointless — domination of nature. Apart from Dan's vineyards, most of the arable land was rented out to a farmer who specializes in cash crops, mainly corn and soya beans. One true pleasure in Harold's retirement years had been to watch somebody else struggle to make a living from the land he had worked most of his life. Even after he'd given up farming, he took a fatalistic attitude. Good weather was always on the verge of breaking, bad weather never came as a surprise, disaster being a farmer's default position.

The funeral "after party" took place on Harold's beloved lawn. Lance estimated two hundred people at the peak. The weather was perfect, a dazzling blue day with a breeze off the lake. The lads' pick-up band soon turned into a jam session with a dozen musicians chiming in. Guests helped themselves to tubs of steaming corn on the cob while three barbecues turned out burgers and sausages. Judging from the age of the crowd, I suspect few of those present could claim to have known the deceased well, if at all. Ginny was the centre of attention. She passed out beers and sang with the band. She even took a turn on Glenn's drums when he ducked away to eat. It seems they'd all been chatting back and forth on Facebook or whatever. This was only a real-life chapter in friendships they'd been keeping up for ages. I was happy to see her slip so easily back into the family, after years of being kept at a distance. Shame on me, I was glad her mother, my difficult sister, Jean, had not chosen to attend.

By nine, the mosquitoes hit. Most people went home. Hard-core party animals moved on to a pub in Picton, while the rest of us retreated inside. Dan produced an unopened bottle of whisky from Harold's precious stash. In Harold's day no one would have dared touch the Canadian Club without permission. Dan would never have asked, knowing the answer would be a grumbling statement of fact: You don't need it. As he passed around shots, I noticed him eye the smoker, an heirloom handed down from the days of Alford and Alice. Lance and I are small-boned, like Harold; Jean and Dan are tall, like our mother, as if two parents split their genes: a boy and a girl each. I wondered how their other attributes had been divvied up. And who would dominate now that they were gone. Lance sat comfortably in the smoker, which was far too small for

Dan. Edie curled up on the sofa and tucked a quilt around her legs; I joined her on the other end. After a long day spent making conversation, our small gathering felt like a refuge. I was proud of Frank for stepping out of the shadows and giving Harold a rousing Celtic send-off. Maybe the Irish in us wasn't dead after all. Maybe it skipped a generation.

I took a sip. The amber liquid burned. I felt like a rebellious teenager, a good feeling, until Edie asked about my eye.

My eye? My face. My whole body ached, though I'd just about forgotten until she brought it up. When Lance lamented the loss of my vintage Mini Cooper, Dan sneered, said I was damn lucky to be alive.

In an effort to turn the conversation away from my faults, I asked Lance whether he was planning to move into Jean's room. If so, we'd have to move her stuff.

He said, What makes you think I'd do that?

Well, you brought quite a lot of luggage. Are you planning a move?

Edie looked at Lance, then over to me. Ms. Bad Poker Face knows everything first. Lance shifted his weight in the smoker, crossed his legs. He said he was done with Vancouver, on the move, so to speak. Dan's eyebrows shot up. Settling in the County?

Lance laughed. Ha! I wouldn't go that far, he said.

Edie launched into a vivid defense of "The New County," pointing out how many fine dining establishments, B&Bs, and pricey shopping spots had sprung up to accommodate the people who came for the vineyards and beaches. All the hard work and trial and error of local viticulture was paying off, she said. Prince Edward County had turned into a true hotspot of culinary and artistic excellence. Internationally known … the hospitality industry … she went on until Lance interjected to ask Dan about the vineyard. What was he planning to do with it now?

Dan ignored the question, instead began to praise the latest vintage, which had won a prize, and offered to open a bottle. Lance said mixing grapes and rye was a bad idea this late in the day. He promised to prepare a meal worthy of celebration as soon as we were in the mood. Then he got up, started clearing the dishes. Dan and Edie went home.

As I climbed the stairs, the ancient treads squeaked under every step, as if footsteps from my battered body caused them pain. My room at the end of the hall hadn't changed much since the day I left home for university, an ungodly number of years ago. The closet was bulging with cast-off clothes, sentimental paperbacks, random memorabilia from growing up on the farm. Dan's and Lance's rooms were spartan. Jean's room was piled to the ceiling with boxes she'd sent home when her marriage broke up a decade ago and she moved "temporarily" to Africa.

Home. Did I just now utter the word? Still calling the old homestead home, after so many years. What does that say about me? At the time of Dad's death, home was a slippery concept. An aging parent had been a duty that pulled me back, then sent me away. An unexamined pattern. When I was in the County, I thought of Toronto as home, but once there, the lines blurred.

4

After the party broke up, Ginny and the boys went to a bar. She ended up spending the night at Dan and Edie's. We'd hardly had occasion to exchange more than a few words until the day after the funeral, when Lance brought her to the farm. Her luggage, lost in the turmoil of a missed flight, arrived by courier — three enormous suitcases. I offered to make space in her mother's room, but she took one look, closed the door, and unpacked her bags in Dan's old room, which was empty except for the bed. Lance had gone off to help the lads return empties; we had the kitchen to ourselves. Ginny used his fancy equipment to make espresso. Normally, I take coffee black but she'd heated milk, so we each had steaming bowls of café au lait. A taste she'd acquired in Europe, she said. She'd have nothing else at breakfast for the rest of her life.

An elegant, confident twenty-two-year-old, Virginia Gupta looked out of place sitting at the old kitchen table, yet she acted completely at home. Genetic connection is a strange force, the fusion of familiar and its opposite. She'd always been so unlike any of us, more worldly, even at the age of ten, big pink ribbons adorning her pigtails, fingers alight with glittering nail polish, lip gloss before she was old enough for colour. Now her style was hypernatural, fashionably wholesome but far from casual. She was wearing tattered jeans that fit like gloves, a white linen blouse, and stylish leather sandals.

A graduate of French immersion high school, she had taken a liberal arts degree in Calgary and spent a semester in Switzerland polishing her French. As Edie had reported, she was planning to be a writer, and she paid me a slew of compliments, including credit for her decision. Finally, the big news: She won a scholarship to pursue an M.A. at Concordia University and would be moving to Montreal in the fall. She'd been planning to come east anyway, even if her grandfather hadn't died. She'd been on the verge of getting in touch when the news came.

An M.A. Well, I said, I thought you wanted to write?

I do. It's the Margaret Laurence Creative Writing Scholarship. I'll be writing a novel as my thesis. I've got full funding for two years.

I'd heard of such programs, the vast industry of creative writing schools that had sprung up since I entered the trade in the eighties. In those days would-be writers went to university in order to read the greats and meditate upon their genius, extract wisdom for use later, discreetly. University taught one how to live a full life. As for writing, my generation believed the power and skills needed to do so were obtained by osmosis. You read, you wrote, you wept, crumpled, rewrote, and eventually turned out a publishable novel. Or you gave up and never talked about it again. In my twenties, I knew quite a few aspiring writers. The whole endeavour was soaked in mystery and taboo. People who talked too much or telegraphed ambition were ridiculed. Talent was a mystery, a gift. Writing was a sacred mission, a cult activity. You could never be sure of the rules, or of who was in and who was out. You would only show a manuscript to a trusted mentor or a close friend.

Evidently, times have changed. I tried to summon enthusiasm, without contradicting my opinion.

Full funding to read literature and write? That's quite something. Congratulations!

I assured her she would love Montreal. It is a wonderful city for young people. She leapt on the subject, wanting to hear all about my McGill years, what it was like to be in Montreal during the Quiet Revolution. That was before my time, I said. Although I do think the so-called revolution has been overdramatized, possibly for political reasons. Woodstock was arguably of greater historical and cultural significance.

No matter, Ginny had formed her own opinions, insisted it must have been an exciting time to live in Montreal.

To tell you the truth, I didn't often read newspapers in those days, I said. I was dating a musician from Vermont. The English department at McGill was a bit of a bubble. It was easy to avoid local politics. If you want the full scoop on Quebec, ask our cousin Myra. She moved to Montreal to be near the political epicentre of the country. She's the family radical.

She sighed, said we had such an interesting family. She was looking forward to getting to know us all again. Now that I'm more mature, she said, I'm ready to appreciate this family. I only wish we hadn't fallen out of touch. It's so unfair.

If I'd been more confident about where Jean and I stood, I might have taken the opportunity to clear the air. But I just did not know how to begin. As we talked, I realized the adults in Clan Cameron existed for Ginny as faces in the photo albums. When she was a child, Jean and Ravi had spent quite a few holidays on the farm, usually in summer, and a couple of chaotic Christmas visits. She had vague memories of Harold and none of her grandmother.

I asked if she'd been published. Yes, a few stories and poems in little magazines (none I'd heard of), mostly written when she was in Switzerland, at what I gathered was some kind of finishing school — at least not a degree-granting institution. She'd won the writing scholarship on the basis of an outline for a novel. She wanted to know what I thought of the plan.

Well. I said that as far as I knew, films get written from outlines, or pitches, not literary novels. If it's genre you're after, probably best to start with a list of plot points and fill in the blanks. But don't listen to me. I said she was lucky to have funding and it would be great to have her in "The East."

Maybe you could read my outline and give me some feedback, she said brightly. She'd been hoping we'd have a chance to talk so she could work up the courage to ask. Would you? I'd be so grateful.

Her request caught me off guard. I danced my way around it, assuring her the outline was no doubt fine as is. My advice: Jump in, write your novel. Don't muddy the process by talk. And don't be discouraged if the first draft is awful. Second, third, fourth drafts are what count. Writing a novel is a solitary adventure.

She looked dismayed. For a moment I hoped she might be about to withdraw the request. No such luck.

Aunt Milly, I really would like to know what you think, *before* I plunge in. I could get Uncle Dan to print out a copy. I've got it on my memory stick.

I gave her my email address, told her to send a digital attachment. No sense wasting paper.

The next morning she took the train to Montreal. Lance drove me to Toronto in Harold's car. He had people to see. I imagined he craved the blessed anonymity of the city. I know I did.

5

You often hear writers claim they "always wanted to write novels." Not me. From the age of consciousness, I set my sights on finding a life beyond the known. I wanted to get off the farm, fill the void of ignorance, and conquer a city, which meant acquiring a circle of smart friends who gathered in bars and posed for black-and-white photographs that would someday be iconic. The actual business of working remained vague. Having drifted into the land of dead white males, I planted my flag in the seventeenth century, won a Dean's medal, and stayed on at McGill for an M.A. thesis on the great god Milton. The obvious next step was a Ph.D. Under the tutelage of a Princeton-educated scholar, I landed a prestigious research grant, which is how I ended up at Oxford, ready to explore the various meanings of fire in *Paradise Lost.* My plan was to get the doctorate, then find an academic post.

On my first weekend trip down to London, I met and fell madly in love with a left-wing activist poet from Aberdeen. For the better part of a year, my life was a manic rhythm of ecstasy and despair. He had fled Scotland with a suitcase full of poems, hoping to find a London publisher. Instead, Margaret Thatcher's austerity campaign galvanized his energies. By the time we met, he'd rallied a circle of angry socialists dedicated to resisting the Tory government's assault on the working class, a heritage of which he was proud. They read Franz Fanon, wore Che Guevara T-shirts, and spent hours arguing over strategy, all terribly exciting, just the kind of edgy existence I'd imagined living. The invasion of the Falkland Islands — a smokescreen allowing the prime minister to entrench neo-liberal policies — drove the movement into the streets, where violent clashes with police sent many to hospital or jail. At the peak of the crisis, a BBC film crew zoomed in on my poet and me embracing under an umbrella, while more focused rebels in the foreground dove for cover. His long-suffering wife saw the clip on TV and showed up at his bedsit with a small handgun in her purse, a vintage Smith & Wesson inherited from her grandfather, an IRA hero. I backed out of the room. After a few anguished phone conversations, I never saw him again.

In the weeks that followed, between bouts of crying and swilling cheap wine, I scribbled an account of love and loss, the full glory details of our time together, ecstasy and betrayal, along with everything I thought and felt about London, life, literature — a panoply of youthful disillusion and betrayal, raw, uncensored. Even poor old Milton got tossed into the fire of suffering. Burned by life, I could not remember what had inspired me to spend so much time poring over a dead man's words, and said so, boldly. I was devastated, paralyzed, unable to imagine the rest of my existence. I stayed in London, hiding out from the archives. It rained for a month.

In the pit of misery, Barry Keehan knocked on my door. We'd dated briefly at grad school in Montreal, but I didn't take him seriously. An indifferent scholar, he seemed more intent on establishing a reputation for throwing great parties than pursuing a career. For reasons I never quite understood, he kept in touch after graduation, sent me ironic postcards, called at Christmas. Somehow he found me in London, at the pit of my blues, living in a cheap rooming house in Soho, thin as a pencil and too weak to resist company of any kind. In the context of a vast foreign city, gossip about McGill classmates and professors, our shared critique of all things Canadian, created an easy intimacy. When he set about seducing me, I assured him my heart was permanently broken. He shouldn't interpret nonresistance as genuine interest. He claimed he didn't care, the metaphysical heart was not an essential organ. Many people get along quite nicely without one. I decided to take him at his word. Between languorous afternoons in my closet of a room, we sat in pubs and drank the last of my scholarship fund.

Finally, on the verge of bankruptcy, I landed a job editing a Canadian professor's manuscript, which required my presence in her office. Barry was broke and had to go home. In the meantime, he'd found time to read my furious typing, which he declared was a novel. He made no prescient comments that

I can recall but offered to show it to an editor in Toronto. I was flattered to think my scribbling might have some poetic merit, but hardly invested hope. Three months later, I got a thick envelope containing four single-spaced pages of notes from Barry, along with an offer of publication from McClelland & Stewart. I did another draft and sent it off. A month later, he sold the manuscript to a prestigious U.K. publisher. A year later I was a published author.

The *Guardian* review was dithyrambic — voice of a generation, lyric masterpiece, etc. — and a string of influential critics concurred. The modest Canadian and U.K. advances were trumped by a hefty American deal and a film option, followed by translations into a dozen languages. The movie came out under another title, with a famous actress playing me. Little that I could recognize as my work appeared on screen, but I made a lot of money. The doctoral thesis deadline passed. Letters from McGill went unopened.

At the age of twenty-seven, I was famous for a novel I could hardly remember writing. The truth is, I had — and still have — no love for that book. I did not believe it stacked up against the great novels of our time. A page turner, breathless momentum, but no depth, no theme or awareness of context. Since that accidental beginning, I've struggled for decades to write a better book — innovative, deep, worthy of the form. In my own estimation, I have come close to succeeding. At least I've stayed with the mission. But in the world of literature and the public eye, I'm still the author of one commercial sensation, a torrent of undigested emotion bereft of meaning. My heartbreak book was not to my literary taste. But I was stuck with it, unable to be another kind of writer.

Erosion was a hurricane that swept through my life, leaving me perched on a precipice. The title paid homage to a poem by E.J. Pratt, one of Canada's leading poets between the wars. In retrospect, a cringeworthy choice, but at the time my heart craved dark matter. I can still recite Pratt's lines from memory:

> It took the sea a thousand years,
> A thousand years to trace
> The granite features of this cliff,
> In crag and scarp and base.
>
> It took the sea an hour one night,
> An hour of storm to place
> The sculpture of these granite seams
> Upon a woman's face.

On the strength of his success with *Erosion*, Barry founded The Keehan Literary Agency, which went on to discover and represent many of Canada's finest writers. I was able to pay cash for a house in Cabbagetown. A tiny house on a double lot, a storey and a half with teal-blue siding, ornate white trim, a picket fence, and patches of garden front and back, plus a decrepit garage at the side.

• • •

By the time I returned from the funeral, the purple sage was in bloom. My tenant in the basement suite had locked the front door and taken in newspapers that piled up in my absence. A few shingles had blown off the porch, a reminder it needed repair, preferably before winter. After the gloomy atmosphere of the farmhouse, my little haven felt like heaven.

There was a message on the answering machine from Delores, Barry's executive assistant. A petite Haitian with a voice like soft ice cream, she always makes an invitation to interact with the Great Man sound like you've won the lottery. I called back, she said he wanted to see me as soon as possible. We agreed on 10:00 a.m. the following day.

Hanging up, I noted two significant points: My agent did not come to the phone and he did not invite me to lunch, which sounded like he had bad news. I dug out the latest draft of my novel-in-progress and settled down in the garden to give it a quick re-read, in case he actually wanted to talk about the manuscript. Unlikely, but I always prefer to be prepared.

In the early years, the Keehan Agency's offices were located in a lovely turn-of-the-century mansion on a residential street near the University of Toronto. A few years ago, Barry cashed in on the property boom and moved into a rented suite in a Bay Street skyscraper. I told him I thought this gave the wrong signal to writers, suggesting the agency was making gobs of money from our ever-declining advances. Barry said sending signals to authors wasn't what agenting was about; the firm needed to be close to the city's corporate heartbeat in order to save us all from penury.

I didn't take much notice at the time, but the new, improved Keehan Inc. was about to veer into ancillary adventures that would have little to do with actual books. They kept a lawyer on retainer and shared space with some nebulous internet concern whose activity was not obvious from the corporate logo. Taking the elevator up to the twenty-second floor gave me vertigo. I was kept waiting in the lobby for twenty-eight minutes, long enough to become thoroughly discouraged by an article in a literary trade magazine by a well-established fiction writer explaining why he spent years sweating over the biography of a famous dead Canadian — because the literary novel is finished, he said. People don't read them anymore. Publishers had lost the ability to make real novels seem important to the book-buying market.

What did he mean by "seem" important? That novels aren't, really, but should be made to appear important? Isn't he really talking about hype, the province of supermarket bestsellers? I hadn't quite finished the article when Delores summoned me into the inner sanctuary.

Barry leapt up from the desk, threw his arms out wide (we do not hug in business situations), and demanded to know where I'd been. He'd been trying to reach me all week.

Sturdy, broad-shouldered, unfailingly well-dressed, a ruddy complexion that telegraphs energy, thick sandy hair sprinkled with grey, my agent at work has great presence, especially in a crowd of strangers. On his own in a professionally decorated office suite, he's a bit much. I didn't feel up to exchanging more platitudes about death, so murmured something vague about being out of town with a friend. He scowled. I knew he expected details — a name, male or female — which were not forthcoming. I always enjoyed his curiosity.

If lacking in warmth and character, Barry's corner office has a spectacular view of Lake Ontario, which he keeps behind his back — unless he has something mean to say, in which case he swivels around and fixes his eyes on the watery horizon. This is a sign meaning "we" will have to take the long view of success and not throw temper tantrums that might involve fragile desk ornaments. He had last used the tactic on me three years earlier, in reference to an early draft of the very novel we were meeting to discuss. A horizon moment for sure: He hated it and twisted himself into knots to avoid saying so.

Since then I'd done a complete rewrite. I was encouraged by the sight of his bulky presence standing in wait. He directed me to a comfortable chair on the other side of the massive imitation Louis XIV table that served as a desk. My manuscript lay in front of him.

I sat down. Smiling broadly, he said he had great news: *Habemus publicam*, heh, heh … we have a publisher. I was confused. I thought we already had a publisher.

So we have a contract? Is that what you're saying?

I'm placing you with a new house, he said. A dynamic young enterprise with a CEO who thinks you're the cat's pyjamas.

You got me out of my contract with …? I named the publisher. He laughed.

Whenever Barry is about to say something outrageous, you can expect a volcanic eruption of mirth designed to lighten the mood by inducing the listener to laugh along. This laughter often has nothing to do with anything funny. The noise died down, he shook his head.

Forget the past. We don't need to worry. These guys aren't Canadian.

What are they?

He laughed again, less forcefully.

Snag Books. A new group, young. Ebooks, audio, print on demand simultaneously. Really kick-ass, cutting edge, trendy as hell. You have to meet them. You will. They're the future of books, Amelia. And they're impressed as hell by the prospect of snagging a writer like you. Heh heh, pun intended.

What?

Snag.

Oh.

He leaned forward to whisper, They print in India.

Snag Books?

The name sounds odd to us. But what do we know, eh? We're old. Their logo's amazing. It's a rubber claw. I have a great deal of confidence in these boys. They'll go far.

Where are they located?

Nowhere.

What?

Nowhere!

Isn't that a small town in the Prairies?

No! I mean literally NOWHERE. They do not have offices. They're a completely virtual enterprise, with a global business plan and deep cybermentality. Futuristic as hell.

I wondered if this could be a joke, but nobody has ever accused Barry Keehan of having a sense of humour about his business. His laughter is strategic. When he gets a piece of juicy gossip about a competitor's troubles, he can be truly hilarious. But not — no, never — about his own cause. I decided to pursue the proposal logically.

Nowhere. Okay. Where did you meet them?

Frankfurt.

The book fair?

He threw his head back, roared. That dying circus? No, the airport. I was changing planes. Delores fucked up. I had a six-hour layover. So did they, going the other way. Heh heh. Amelia, these guys have many, many, many irons in the fire. Novels are — what can I say — their *Violin d'Ingres.*

When Barry starts dropping French phrases into a conversation, I get nervous. It's like watching Pinocchio's nose expand before your eyes. Usually, it means he's lying to himself. He's a fantastic salesman. His great strength is self-delusion. He actually believes the tales he spins, and his belief is contagious. In circumstances such as this, truth had to be stalked and cornered. I peppered him with questions: When and where will my book be coming out? What is the promotion plan? And how much will we be getting as an advance?

The chair began to swivel.

I raised my voice: Barry, do NOT turn and face the lake!

He turned back, loosened his tie. I believe he only puts on a tie in the morning so that he can loosen it strategically to let writers believe they're making him sweat, instead of the other way around. Then he picked up my manuscript and held it, like a cake, between us. In a low, faintly patronizing tone, he said, Of course we have a pub date. August first next year, in time for the awards if we pull up our socks. The promotion campaign will be massively online. YouTube, Twitter or whatever it is, Facebook, Instagram, *HuffPo*, *Slate*, Tumblr, and a gazillion other more important platforms neither you nor I have heard of, because they have yet to be invented. But they will be, in time for your novel. And you will be big. Not just this (the manuscript) but you personally. I predict a full restoration of your career, with royalties to match and international celebrity.

He made the last word into a roller-coaster ride. Ce-leb-bri-tee. Then he dropped my manuscript, with a thud.

I asked for precision on the size of the advance.

No advance. He spit out the words, as if the very idea was some kind of Victorian anachronism.

I stood up. Walked over to the window. Stared at the lake.

This is not good, I said.

Amelia, this is the future. Advances are a thing of the past. You know full well an advance is only a loan against future profits. You're borrowing from yourself. Who falls for that?

No, Barry. An advance is payment for years of unremunerated labour. It's proof that a publisher intends to do all those things that sell books. It is their investment in my work.

Yada, yada, yada. Look, I'm not getting a penny up front either. I'm doing this out of appreciation for your life's work. I want to see you continue to flourish as a serious literary writer, and succeed in a brutal new marketplace. Tall order!

He was standing behind me. I glared at our reflection in the window: two aging Canadians who had once enjoyed furious sex in London, now wedded to our work, a pair of old coats, out of style, diminished, limp, hoping for a few more winters. I'm not going to cry over money, I said, struggling to convince myself.

Money is a perfectly good reason to cry, he replied, putting a hand on my shoulder. We will make money. Listen, the book business is in a tailspin, Amelia. I know you don't follow the financial news, but I'm sure you're up on the gossip. Everybody's going bust, except a few at the very top, and they're all horizontally integrated. It's hellishly complicated.

But my book *is* coming out on paper, with covers back and front?

Yes. He gulped.

And it will be available in Toronto?

Silence.

Barry?

Of course it will be available in Toronto, and everywhere else on planet Earth! That's the world we live in. I'm just not sure of the precise local timeline. We do have a few legal issues with the past, you know. Stuff to wrap up. You personally will see paper copies of your book, if I have to get them FedExed from Delhi myself.

Delhi? I glanced at the five-hundred-page manuscript on his desk, imagined my book stranded in India. The heat. The flies. I could not believe anyone over there would give a fiddler's damn. And who in Canada would even hear about it?

He looked mystified.

Who's going to read my book? I whined. It made me wince.

Everybody, eventually. These new distribution routes take time to work up. We're on the frontier. Have faith in me, as I have faith in you. And your writing.

Is there anything to sign? I asked meekly, once again putting my fragile ego in his hands. His voice dropped. He was standing close, practically whispering in my ear.

Premature. Go home and give it one last polish. You might want to trim it a tad.

What? Cut it down? Barry, please!

Okay, okay, shoot me the final draft attachment by Monday.

Monday? No! Impossible. You know how a publishing contract focuses the mind. Maybe by Christmas.

Thanksgiving at the latest. He looked at his desk calendar: Friday, October 12. Noon. He wrote my name on the page.

I looked around his office. A large painting by a local wunderkind whose work sells in the five-figure range hung over an Italianate sofa. Two matching armchairs echoed the startling colours of the painting. On a glass coffee table were copies of *The Globe and Mail* and *Wall Street Journal*. The environment created by a top designer included a mini-bar, a stereo system, and a widescreen TV. No books. I imagined the agency's fifteen percent from my last novel had been enough to pay for a couple of throw cushions. I flattered myself. Maybe one. I asked for the Snag website address, hoping to convey enthusiasm.

He shook his head. Wouldn't do you much good. They're still too cutting edge.

No website? Virtual publishers living nowhere? Will the text be set in invisible ink? I did not have a good feeling about this news, although Barry sounded positive. He's such a terrific salesman. He can make an insecure author feel good in a downpour.

He straightened his tie, buttoned his jacket, steered me toward the door. An extremely beautiful young Asian woman was waiting at reception. He introduced us: Hope Shung-Lee, first-time author of a sizzling novel called *Ravished*, which he'd just signed with the Random House conglomerate.

She grew up right here in Mississauga, he gushed. We're handling world rights.

They headed out for lunch.

I went straight home. I had to lie down. I don't cope well with change. A few years earlier, I'd been through a comparable nightmare when Barry engineered the transfer from my international trade publisher to a smaller, now defunct literary house based in Winnipeg. He'd convinced me a "boutique" enterprise would be a better match for my "kind of writing." I remember the day he broke the news.

You're a body-of-work writer, he explained over dinner. You're not a flavour-of-the-month. You tackle the big picture. Writing is your vocation.

He said the big publishers had all been bought up by international corporations and so were under intense financial pressure. The editors were terribly overworked dealing with thousands of manuscripts that poured in every month. Far too many books were getting published, driven by corporate terror of missing out on the next big thing. He believed I belonged with a publisher/editor who approached the craft at a different pace.

Of course I followed his advice, although I didn't feel particularly good about it. Only later did I find out my original publisher had actually dropped me. I heard it from an insider who'd been sacked and didn't give a damn about the nondisclosure agreement. Barry had found me a new publisher and kept the nasty part to himself. Maybe I should have been grateful. Instead, I was angry. I swore that if I'd known the truth, I'd have fought it. *Erosion* is still in print. It's studied in university courses. What more did they want?

Another bestseller, he said.

As a writer, you're never on solid ground when it comes to sales, deals, that sort of thing. The nebulous space between writing and readers is the slaughterhouse. Best not to think about it, and normally I don't. I've never been interested in the politics or mechanics of publishing, as long as my novels found their way into print. Apart from the odd outburst to keep him on his toes, I'm happy to leave the blood and gore to Barry. He thrives on it.

Actually, the true cause of my distress on that hot August day, while my agent was lunching a young sensation, was Tuscany. Every two years, Barry invites his inner circle of friends and writers to his villa near Lucca for a fortnight of revelry. He had mentioned the dates to me in April but had said nothing since. I'd seen him a couple of times at literary events. Now the meeting in his office over the Snags. Silence. Maybe he'd forgotten. No, he hadn't. I remembered past years when he had dropped people, added others. They weren't officially disinvited; he just didn't mention Tuscany.

Too distraught to fall asleep, I attacked the garden, removing bushels of weeds that had sprung up since my sudden departure, and watered the lingering flowers. Going through old emails, I found an invitation to a dinner party at a fellow writer's home. Called him. It wasn't too late. I went to the dinner, ate Tuscan food, commiserated about the death of the novel, drank too much wine, took a cab home, cried, checked my email.

There was a message from Ginny with her scholarship award–winning outline attached. I pressed delete and went to bed.

6

Five years in, my novel-in-progress still didn't have a title. Every time I thought of a good one, it inspired me to rewrite, which is not a good sign. Now I considered the stack of pages with the Snags in mind. I pictured them, thin androgynous beings in shiny jackets over sweatshirts, skinny black pants, and spiky haircuts, sitting in airport lounges bent over their phones. I wondered what they found in my work-in-progress to inspire confidence. I looked at the calendar, counted back from Barry's deadline: only a few weeks, meaning work would have to begin immediately. I opened the file, made a pot of tea, drank a cup, poured another.

A week went by during which I cleaned the house from top to bottom, reorganized my books, opened every piece of junk mail, changed the furniture around, stocked the fridge with healthy foods, obtained estimates for reshingling the roof and made two dozen jars of tomato paste from produce purchased at the St. Lawrence Farmer's Market.

I had just finished steam-sealing the last of the Mason jars on Friday afternoon when Ginny called. She wondered if I'd received her outline. I said I had, but my computer was on the fritz and some messages had gone astray. Could she send it again? She did. I settled down with a glass of Bordeaux from the Mâcon region, 1999, fully intending to open the file.

Just then an important email came in. An academic publishing firm was offering me a rush contract to edit a thesis manuscript. The subject was Troubadour poetry, a new take on romance literature as it relates to folk tales. I accepted immediately, decided to go straight to bed so I could begin in the morning with a clear head.

I've never minded editing work. It's technical, soothing, a nice break from writing, and it pays quite well. The client-editor relationship is based on serving ideas on the page, seeking the clearest possible expression. The ego content is relatively low. I set to work happily. Days flew by in productive silence.

At the end of the second week, I got an email from Ginny, after midnight. I'd crawled into bed with my laptop and forgotten to close down before drifting off. The ping woke me up. She said she was thinking about visiting Toronto, wondered if I'd have time to get together. I noticed she was writing from her phone and called her.

Oh, Aunt Milly, I didn't think you'd be awake. Sorry.

Her voice was feeble, groggy, as if she'd been crying. I asked if there was anything wrong.

She said no. Silence. Then she broke into sobs.

When I asked the reason, her sobs turned into tears, gasps.

Where are you?

M-Montreal.

I mean, where at home?

In bed.

What's the matter?

I don't want to bother you.

You're not bothering me. I'm concerned. Please tell me, why the tears? Did something awful happen?

I thought of all the terrible stories about campus life that make it into the newspapers. Wild sorority parties, binging, drugs. Everybody's in therapy or on prescriptions. An innocent young girl from Calgary walking around the Concordia campus at night, with drunken muscular frats on the prowl. Anything could happen.

She let out a loud sigh, like a groan, then said, I think I've got …

Pause.

What?

Well … (sniff) … writer's block.

Shame on me, I laughed. Nervous laughter, quickly and convincingly turned into a small coughing fit. She asked if I was all right.

Yes, I'm fine. Thanks. You know, Ginny, writing takes time. You can't rush it.

I don't think I can take the pressure. How do you handle it?

I was tempted to blurt out, I don't. My life is one long moan, a litany of deaths and resurrections, delusionary highs and sickeningly familiar lows. But some hitherto unknown force, maybe an untapped reserve of maternal instinct, checked the impulse to speak honestly. The alternative was platitudes. We talked for what seemed like hours. Or, rather, I listened as she related stories of difficult professors, impossible assignments, troublesome conversations with fellow "writers," doubts about the outline, the physical effects of worry, sleeplessness, stomach pains, a nasty rash. Her anxiety was contagious. Like those awful moments before throwing up, I had to take deep breaths. Finally, in a desperate attempt to end the conversation, I said it might be a good idea if she came to Toronto. We could talk at leisure, maybe catch a movie, eat dinner in a restaurant.

Really, you think so?

If you can spare the time, I said, disguising hope for a reprieve in the form of a hint.

She blew her nose. Her voice cleared. She hung up in a cheerful mood, with a train time punched into her phone calendar. I slumped back into the pillows, completely winded. According to the bedside clock, I'd been on the phone just under thirty minutes. The sun was not about to rise. Clearly, the role of mentor was harder than I imagined. Fortunately, I'd had the presence of mind to leave time before Ginny's arrival for my only paid activity that month. I could finish the edit, if I did nothing but work until the doorbell rang.

She arrived late Friday afternoon bearing bagels, smoked salmon, and a great bottle of French wine. The taxi driver carried her shiny pink suitcase up my front porch stairs and deposited it in the hallway, the first time I'd experienced that level of service. When she thanked him, he blushed and even without a tip, wished her a pleasant stay in Toronto. Such is the power of youth and beauty.

I had prepared a light supper. We opened her wine and after eating moved into the living room with decaf espresso and shots of liqueur. Conversation revolved around her social life in Montreal, which sounded more hectic than she'd implied on the phone. As we settled into comfy chairs by the gas fireplace, I ventured into the subject of writing. How is it going?

It isn't, she said, in a resolute, not entirely cheerless tone. To tell you the truth, I've faced my doubts about the program. It's so, so clear. Whew! I made a mistake.

What do you mean?

I get a woozy feeling just walking through the halls. Is this where I need to be? I mean, at this point in my life? Yuck. What was I thinking? I quit.

But you've only been there a month.

Six weeks feels like forever. I keep thinking of what you said. Will I ever be a writer if I spend a year or two or three *talking about writing*? No, I won't. You were so, so right. Ugggh!

I did not remember having verbalized my reservations so bluntly. I pointed out that the Margaret Laurence Scholarship was a great opportunity, as well as a substantial sum of money for someone her age.

I would never make a decision based on money, she declared. That's just not the way I intend to live my life.

She's only twenty-two, I had to remind myself. Everybody thinks that way at her age, not only girls with wealthy fathers, fashion model poise, and taxi drivers ready to kiss their hemlines. She was stretched out on the chaise lounge, wearing a white silk kimono that set off her black hair. I stifled a yawn, hoped she would say or do something sympathetic to stave off my desire for sleep. Or take the hint and suggest bed.

She sat upright, hands on her knees, and said, It's the outline. The outline is complete shit. I'm sure you agree. Be honest.

An awkward moment, to be sure. I had heard her talk about the outline but, indeed, had not glanced at the document, although there were two copies and several follow-up emails on my computer. I had promised to read it. I was being tested and was about to fail, miserably. I do not like the taste of failure. It's worse than telling a lie. So I said, Look, Ginny, I'm going to be honest. I purposely did not read your outline. I was afraid … I feared any response might sully your inspiration. Writing fiction is a personal quest. It's … fragile. You know I believe in you. But you have to find the confidence to continue within yourself. The novel is *in* you, Ginny. Getting it *out* must be your solitary mission. Do not be distracted by ersatz midwives who promise otherwise.

She got up, knelt in front of me, and wept. I do not choose the synonym for crying carelessly: long black hair draped over my lap, shoulders heaving, hot tears splashing on my bare knees. I felt like I was sitting onstage during an opera.

You are so … so right, she wailed. She straightened up and looking at me with shimmering brown eyes, cheeks aglow, said, Aunt Amelia, that is the most important statement I've heard about writing — ever. You have saved me from drowning in the murky hell of a creative writing degree.

I said I hadn't meant she should quit the program. On the contrary. I meant there are always obstacles to be met head on. She wasn't listening. She began pacing in front of the fire. In my miniature living room her paces amounted to no more than three steps, which meant she was virtually going around in circles.

Waving her arms, she declared everything was crystal clear. She would quit Concordia, move to Toronto.

I tried to calm her down. What was I babbling? She was incredibly calm. I was the one gripped by panic.

Before I had a chance to extol the legendary creative energy of Montreal, or bemoan the hideous cost of living in Canada's economic capital, she changed the subject.

You didn't read the outline. I respect that. But I feel it's important to ascertain your judgment and make an objective decision about the future of this novel. Trust me, Aunt Amelia, I am strong enough to accept your comments. I respect you deeply. I feel we share the same creative DNA. If you hate it, I'll find another story. I need to face up to the truth, and move on.

She disappeared upstairs to get her outline, came down wearing sweatpants and a baggy sweater, sleeves rolled up, her hair tied back in a ponytail. I poured a second round of Grand Marnier, never a great idea but sometimes essential, and sat back in the armchair, braced myself for the award-winning summary of a novel she was determined to call *Road Trip*.

The actual text, which she waved as she spoke, has been lost to posterity, deleted from my computer later in a moment of fury. There's a good chance Ginny did the same. I don't know. But the facts as presented by her that night are seared into my subconscious. It was a story of heartbreak, loss, reconciliation. A young girl caught up in the maelstrom of her parents' exploding marriage. The plot centred on the girl's journey across the United States by several modes of transportation, pursued by her father, who has a dark secret to reveal, one which puts the troubled marriage in context, justifies his regretful behaviour, and ultimately sets his daughter on her life path. It was funny, detailed, poignant, tear-inducing. Bordering on unbelievable, perhaps slipping below the border — hard to tell — so vivid was her recitation. It struck me that she belonged in the theatre. She lived every moment, including the climax. The father (who is Black) and daughter (mixed race) are caught up in a massive street demonstration, inner city Georgia, protesting the killing of four young black boys by police and the subsequent sham investigation, which absolved the offending police officers of wrongdoing. Meanwhile, back home, the girl's mother sees her soon-to-be ex-husband and daughter in a TV clip, being badly roughed up in the melee, and takes the next flight to Georgia. The confrontation, in a seedy hotel room, brings the marriage plot to a fiery finale. The parents have their final showdown; the daughter pulls them back from the brink. The collision of humour and pathos was riveting, breathtaking, bordering on ridiculous.

Before I had time to formulate a response, she stopped abruptly, crumpled the pages, and tossed them in the direction of the fire. I leaned over and grabbed them. Why? Posterity? An irrational fear that gas flames might somehow penetrate the glass and cause damage to the carpet? I don't remember.

Well, I said. That's one hell of a story.

I hate it, she snarled.

You can't hate it. You wrote it.

Yes, I can, she said. I'm like that. When I turn on something, be it a person or my own creation, I don't look back.

She poured herself three inches of sweet orange-flavoured nectar and downed it in one gulp.

The next day being Saturday, Ginny slept until noon. Over eggs Benedict, I mentioned a few museums and places of interest she might like to visit. Or we could go to a play. There was always shopping. She said the Royal Ontario Museum sounded perfect, and a play would be just the thing to take her mind off writing. First, she had to shower, do makeup, and decide what to wear. It was late afternoon when we left the house, with hardly enough time to check out the sales at Bloor and Yonge before grabbing a sandwich and heading to the theatre.

The play was a savage comedy by a popular French writer about two couples, parents of boys, who squabble over an injury inflicted on one kid by the other. The action takes place at one couple's home over a single, long visit. No children in sight, plenty of liquor, little to propel the plot forward besides the gradually released inner turmoil of four well off urbanites whose civil veneer is extremely thin. At first, I resisted the play's too-obvious architecture but was soon swept up by great performances, sharp dialogue, and a delirious audience. With the exception of a gasp-worthy puking scene, it was all talk-talk-talk, slick and raw. Far from the subterranean depths of prose fiction wherein I spend my writing life. Bordering on vulgar, contrived and yet utterly alive. I'm more of a movie person than a theatregoer. I prefer the distance of film. Plays tend to be invasive, faintly embarrassing. This one was open warfare. I loved it.

Afterward, I wanted nothing more than to take a long walk alone, savour the atmosphere. But Ginny was bursting with commentary. She said she'd read the script and found the production compelling. Wasn't the whole thing just wicked? Shouldn't *Road Trip* have the same bark and bite?

We were standing in the courtyard lobby as the buzzing audience moved toward the door. I was still in the mood of the play, unable to speak. As we reached the street, I felt a tap on my shoulder and turned around. It was Barry. He gave me a bear hug and smiled warmly at Ginny.

I said I hadn't known he was a theatre person.

I'm on the board, he said, as if presenting an excuse. Remind me to sell you a subscription.

He was looking at Ginny as he spoke. I introduced them: my niece, a writer; my agent. An electric moment. I don't remember precisely how the conversation went, but by the end we'd agreed to be his guest for brunch the following day, at a downtown terrace café.

Barry and Ginny ordered salade niçoise and white wine. I had beef tartare and a glass of Burgundy. Barry held forth with his favourite celebrity anecdotes in which he plays a central role. Ginny listened attentively, laughed in all the right places, interjecting only to establish her admiration.

Finally, he turned the subject around, asking about her favourite writers. Her list met with his approval: Dave Eggers, Sheila Heti, Nelly Arcan, Margie Lapone (Barry's discovery), with a smattering of classics and foreigners, as far as I can remember: Colette, Houellebecq, Banana Yoshimoto. Barry assured her that Houellebecq fell flat in translation. And wasn't he a ripe old misogynist anyway?

Ginny protested, she'd read him in the original: He's the Holden Caulfield of his generation. I mean, pretty cynical, yes. But on trend and, underneath, a romantic. What I really, really admire is his honesty.

Barry was enchanted, as if admiring honesty was a radical new idea. He asked about her writing. She blushed, shot me a glance, declared she was working on a novel. At least, the hard part: writing it.

He laughed. Send it to me when you've got a draft. Even an outline. Writers are getting healthy advances on one-pagers these days. What's your story? Please tell me it's set in India.

Sensing she was actually about to answer, I reminded him it's unwise to talk about a work-in-progress. He nodded, changed the subject back to Ginny.

So Amelia, you never mentioned you had a lovely and talented niece? Why not?

Ginny blushed. I said something about her studying in Europe, we'd lost touch.

Barry said he could never understand how family members lose touch.

But then I'm an only child, practically an orphan. My old man was rarely in the picture. My mother's a witch. No blood relations. Or even blood. She sprang fully formed from the mind of a mad Romanian scientist.

Well, the Camerons are a really great family, Ginny said (deftly ignoring his attempt at humour). At least that's what I discovered at Grandpa's funeral. I'm not going to get out of touch, ever again. Right, Aunt Milly?

Barry laughed. Aunt Milly. That's cute. Wait a minute, your grandpa's funeral? Amelia, does this mean your father died?

I nodded.

When? His expression clouded over.

August. Civic holiday weekend.

Why didn't you call me? I'd have gone to the funeral. How did he die? Was he ill?

Not that we know of, I murmured. He fell off the roof.

Oh, Christ. That's awful. I can't believe Harold Cameron is dead, such a vital human being. He hung his head.

Barry, you met him once.

He made an impression. Amelia Cameron, are we close or not?

I'm sorry. I was … you know, it all happened quite quickly.

You're still in shock, he said, reaching for my hand.

Time to go, I said. Ginny has a train to catch.

He picked up the bill, pulled me aside as Ginny headed out the door.

Why didn't you call me? I would have been there for you.

He had that familiar wounded set to his face, as if I'd stomped on his feelings. In my defence, I had been in a state of shock, too dazed to imagine telling anyone. Especially Barry, who is so unfailingly full of feelings needing to be expressed. I could not have faced his love of emotional drama, or his sentimental notions of how families operate.

• • •

After lunch with a bona fide agent, Ginny's enthusiasm for writing seemed to recover. She said she had another idea for a novel. One with less plot, more atmosphere. She might be able to lift parts of *Road Trip*, but basically, she was going to start typing and see what came out. Maybe the real problem had been too much structure. Writing the outline destroyed her creative instinct. What did I think? I mumbled something about being sure she could work through issues of process and shouldn't let anything distract her from the task at hand.

As the taxi pulled up to my front door, she gave me a big hug and a piece of advice, delivered with a warm grin that left me feeling exposed: Call Barry, she said. He seems pretty upset about being left out of the funeral.

Mr. Keehan is my agent, I wanted to say. Agents don't attend family funerals. Instead, I nodded and wished her well.

After collapsing in front of the TV for a spell, I went up to bed. On my way past the guest room I peeked in. It was a mess, as if she'd been living in solitary confinement for months. Mixed up in the bedsheets were a tube of hand cream, a pair of underpants, a bra; under the bed, the current copy of *Vanity Fair* and an empty water bottle. Stacking the leftovers in a pile, I wondered what, if anything, was worth sending to her. The postage would be a small fortune. The magazine was dog-eared, bulky. I flipped it open and found a wad of papers covered with scribbles, obviously written after our conversation about writing. How could she have forgotten her precious notes?

I put the phone on silent in case she decided to call in the middle of the night. She didn't. A few days later an elegant thank you note arrived by post. PS: I forgot some stuff, but no need to send anything. Working on a new idea. *Road Trip* is dead.

• • •

Our semi-business lunch that day turned out to be the beginning of an accidental — I'm tempted to say innocent — literary hoax, but that's not quite true. Let's say we were unaware of the energy our threesome unleashed. Playing the scene in my head now, I am astounded at my ability to record details and, yet at the time, completely fail to grasp their meaning. Ginny telling me to call Barry. Why? She hardly knew either of us. I wondered if she had a crush on him, if he had been swept away by her youth and beauty (not an original story). Never did I suspect they would become tight conspirators. Or that she would instantly see a connection I had ignored for decades, if not ignored, then chose to overlook. Young girls crave love stories. They find them under every rock, whereas women of an age learn to enjoy the comforts of complicated relationships with smooth surfaces. I was lucky she came into my life at just the right moment, or I might have died and gone into obscurity without turning over that particular rock.

7

A TV talk show host once asked me what I did when I wasn't writing. Without thinking, I said procrastinate. Meaning everything but writing is time wasted, distraction. My normal pace is on the slow side, somewhere between adagio and larghetto. I can spend a day on a single paragraph. A sentence might be revised a hundred times before it gets into print. Word order, back and forth. Adjective in, out. Entire chapters, into the bin and back out again. The architecture is fundamental, but it's impossible to settle on structure until the thousand-piece puzzle exists. And then it's almost too much to hold in the mind. Which is what I'd come to expect from the writing life, that it would be almost impossible.

After the easy gratification of editing, followed by a rock 'n' roll weekend with an emerging writer, I was looking forward to getting back to my own work. Until I was actually staring at the stack of typing, then I faced a wave of revulsion. Clearly, it would take time to get back into the world of my novel. I undertook a binge of domestic chores, hoping to cheer myself up, or at least make the effort of writing possible again.

Instead, I confronted a brick wall; this novel will never be finished, should never have been started. Surely, every serious writer has a book that goes nowhere. It's the price you pay for taking risks. I was spoiled; having published five novels to largely positive reviews, I'd been unprepared to flush away years of work. Still, Barry was building a new phase of my career on the basis of this manuscript. His deadline was in front of my face. It would have to be extended. Yet at some level, I did not believe the problem could be solved by more time. A terrifying thought.

While incoherent scenes of failure were swirling around in my head, I also began to worry about Ginny. I felt I'd been too hard on her, yawned at her writer's block. Dismissed her anxieties, even tried to discourage her from taking up the scholarship, and then changed my mind. No wonder the girl was having trouble. I had stumbled into a writing career at a propitious moment, when CanLit was newborn. In retrospect, success was easier then. Ginny not only had thousands of successful writers to compete with for space, but a grouchy aunt who thought she knew something about the art form, yet wasn't writing her own book. Or helping her niece.

I woke up in a sweat one night and wrote her a rambling apology. At 3:00 a.m. it seemed brilliant. The next morning I was revolted, pressed delete.

A few days later, Ginny called. Another meltdown. I was heartened, almost thanked her for offering a second chance to be a better aunt. This time the problem was personalities. She didn't like her fellow students, or the instructors who thought they were gifted. They weren't her kind of people. They played games. They were purposely mean.

What kind of games?

Well, they show off their knowledge, and if somebody else hasn't read some obscure European author, they roll their eyes. Also, I really do not like reading my work in front of people. Reading out loud makes me sick.

Nothing she said surprised me. I was desperate to help her but could not think of a single helpful or even faintly positive response.

Instead, I suggested she take a long walk on Mount Royal. Do that every day. Get good running shoes, pick up the pace. Cut down on sugar and carbs, stay away from liquor. When your head and gut are perfectly clear, the best course of action will be obvious.

A pause. Then she said I was brilliant, she adored me, and would be eternally grateful.

Hanging up, I felt good, except for one niggling concern: I myself had never tried such a strategy — although I sincerely believed it would work.

Why hadn't I given her something more substantial than a pep talk? Or banal advice she could get from the blizzard of self-help books coming out daily, or from her mother for that matter? I thought about calling her back to tell her I was thinking about *Road Trip*. I searched my computer for the outline. Nothing. I'd deleted the attachments along with her emails. Then I remembered the material she'd left behind after the heady brunch with Barry. I dug out the crumpled outline she'd flung at the fire and read it, including her scribbled comments following our conversation. The story had potential. The father, especially, was an interesting character. Weak and whingey at first, almost pathetic, until the hotel scene, when his wife exposes his flaws and he steps up to defend himself, risking his daughter's love in defence of honesty. I'm a flawed human being, he says, if you consider a taste for wearing women's clothing a flaw. Of course there was more, a lot more. Years of ambivalence during which he tried to hide his feminine cravings for the sake of family stability.

The outline was terse, factual, yet the girl's point of view seethed with anger. I could feel the pulse, even in a description. Her telling of the story had been effective. A scene like the hotel encounter between parents and daughter was a mountain peak. All you had to do is get the climbing pace right and avoid dithering or stumbling on the way down. I decided to type up her notes, explain the merit of her idea. This was not an onerous task.

If only I'd been able to stop, press delete, and get back to my own novel. Instead, I wrote furiously, day and night, until there was nothing left to say. Wrote her an email saying take a look at this, maybe it will be of some use. Attached the document, pressed send, and put the matter out of my mind.

Facing up to my role as writing coach worked like a tonic. I got a sudden inspiration on the matter of a title for my own lost tome. *Abstraction*. One-word titles are punchy, elegant. This one had the virtue of being snappy, yet profound. It was cloud-like, mysterious. Perfect for the tale told. Finally, the work stood on its own feet. I resolved to look upon my manuscript coldly, as if the task ahead were an editing job that would pay good money as soon as I met the terms of contract. Working objectively, I was able to remove eighty pages, a feat sure to please Barry and his Snags. I stopped wondering whether it was any good. I just wanted it shorter. On the second pass, I switched from biscuits to raw carrot sticks. Another hundred pages hit the trash.

I felt lighter, as if I had indeed trotted up the mountain and was coming down again.

PART II

Solstice

8

Friends of mine who have a beach house in Barbados invited me to join them for the Christmas holidays, thinking I must be blue about Harold's death and need support. I was set to go until Edie called to talk over the holiday menu. She went on about how we would all have to gather round and make the best of a gloomy season, get through this together, etc. I didn't have the heart to disappoint her. So on December 23, I boarded the train at Union Station, dragging a suitcase full of Camembert and Côtes de Rhône. Lance picked me up in Belleville. He was driving Harold's pickup, wearing a thin fleece jacket and a pair of loafers — still hoping winter was a cold flash and would go away. I had to laugh.

The house smelled different. Whiffs of Pine-Sol cleaner and strong coffee, with an undertone of wood smoke, or maybe it was the absence of smell. The old-man odour of pipe juice was gone. So was half the furniture. Lance seemed to be bending the decor to his own Zen tastes. He'd culled the main floor contents by about half, moved a decrepit rocking chair and china cabinet into the woodshed, vanquished several rickety pressbacks to the cellar. His additions stood out: A handmade Christmas wreath hung on the kitchen door, sheets of plastic duct-taped over the leaky windows, and blanket rolls blocking the gap under drafty doors. The parlour couch and chairs were covered in bedsheets, giving the room an eerie sense of finale, as if important guests had exited, leaving wasted country folk to their tiresome routines. A wood fire was roaring, despite a stiff note in Dan's handwriting prominently tacked to the mantle: Do Not Use Fireplace. Chimney Unsafe.

Lance was standing in the hallway with my suitcase. I pointed to the sign. Did you see the note? He shrugged, said Dan's not in charge of this house in spite of what he seems to think. A decade younger than Jean, Lance has always been eager to make his mark — and quick to take offence. Even a mildly judgmental comment can set him on edge.

In retrospect, his response would stand as our Christmas theme, although at the time it seemed to fit a familiar pattern. Since our mother died, my two brothers had often been at odds. Harold never took sides, said he was too old to meddle in "other people's business," an attitude he extended to Lance. So Dan, the self-appointed patriarch, stepped in to provide a guiding hand. He tried with me, too, but he wasn't part of my life in the city, so I never bothered to take him on.

Lance had left for Vancouver in his early twenties. He kept his visits home short. He seemed to enjoy his youthful bad-boy reputation in the family. On the surface at least, the three of us got along well. Maybe it shored up our confidence to revisit a place where we could be the people we'd once been, with other familiar people who never changed. Maybe we didn't really know each other. Not everybody yearns to be known. I've never quite understood the urge. The stories of strangers interest me greatly, I can't help drawing them out. But squeezing secrets from flesh and blood? Risky. You are stuck forever with the ongoing saga of their turmoil.

When our mother was alive, Christmas was a command performance. You either showed up or produced a good excuse. After she died, I kept up the routine for Harold's sake, at least that's what I told myself, although he never seemed particularly thrilled about all the commotion, tended to nod off in his smoker right after dinner, while we sat around quaffing his liquor and gossiping as if he wasn't there. What I loved most about those revelries was the presence of my nephews Frankie, Glenn, and Tom. Being around them during a major gift-giving event was pure joy. They exuded a level of enthusiasm quite outside my reach. And Edie always went to so much trouble orchestrating outstanding meals. It was a pleasure to put city problems on pause and be swept up in her greeting card image of a big happy family.

• • •

Lance had unpacked the box of nativity figurines and assembled them on the buffet, which had notably escaped the purge. A shabby gaggle, the sheep still famously missing (he'd snatched them away one year to join his farm set), the nativity had been a Christmas ritual in our childhood, along with starting an advent calendar, the countdown to Santa. In the mid-period era of widowed Harold, Lance had insisted on calling them The Palestinians. He kept adding figures from his travels, exotic animals and miniature national dolls, until the assembly resembled something between a zoo and an airport. So I wasn't alone in my love of nostalgia.

A further surprise: He'd prepared a dinner of pork medallions with caramelized apples and red onions served on a bed of wild rice. When I asked what happened to his vegetarian rule, he mumbled something about organic meat being easy to get in the County and actually quite healthy, in moderation. So, the County is rubbing off on you, I teased. He shrugged, said he had to build up some capital before heading south.

The States?

No, the real south: Costa Rica, maybe Argentina. Getting a plan was taking longer than he'd expected.

After dinner we headed to the parlour. I plopped down on the saggy sofa, pulled the wool blanket over my legs. Lance may have fallen off the vegetarian wagon, but he obviously drew the line at fossil fuels. The oil furnace had yet to kick in since the sun went down. Oven heat had taken the edge off dinner at the kitchen table, but the parlour was glacial. The fire had dwindled. There was a huge pile of wood by the fireplace, something that would not have happened in Harold's time. As he plucked a few pieces of kindling and began to build up the flames, I couldn't resist returning to the subject of Dan's warning note. He might be arrogant, but he might also be right.

Relax, he said. The chimney's fine. Anyway, this place is well insured. How much do you think it's worth? At least half a million, and I'm not talking about the rolling hills and timber, or the view. Just the house.

I was shocked to hear him talk that way. How could you put a monetary value on a view? Or this farm, for that matter. Are you saying you hope this house burns down?

He said, It might be the best solution.

Solution to what?

He'd settled back in a brocade wingback, which was now positioned dangerously close to the flames. We were drinking port, a gift left over from a Christmas past. He'd been finding bottles all over the place, tucked away out of sight. Harold wasn't much of a drinker, but he did take care to hoard his stash from visiting pirates. I wondered how long it would take to definitively shake down the old homestead.

All property has a monetary value, Lance said. I know you don't want to hear talk of money. But it's true.

So, you think we should sell the farm?

That's not an option, he said. I was relieved to hear him say it. His face was set in a vague half-smile, but his eyes were not friendly.

Of course things change, always, I said. Life is change. But Camerons have been here since the 1800s. An unbroken chain, so to speak. We can all agree that change, when it comes, should be, well … evolutionary.

And democratic?

Of course! I picked up the bottle of port, refilled my glass. Noticed — in my handwriting scribbled in black ink — to Dad from Amelia, 2004. Well, thank you, me. I offered him a refill. He proffered his glass.

Whoa, Amelia, let me clarify before we get too drunk: There is no question of us selling this place, for one simple reason. Because Dan owns it outright.

What do you mean?

His name is on the deed. Only his name.

How do you know?

I went through Harold's papers. Found the deed and, by the way, the will. He gave the farm to Dan the year he planted his vines. The will was drawn up at the same time. The cash, household contents, and a few stocks go to you, Jean, and me. I suppose you're wondering how much that is? Well, right next to nothing. So there you go. Are you interested in having the couch you're sitting on? By all means, take it.

What about Jean?

Ha! I doubt very much she'll fight you over the couch.

I meant — have you talked to her? Does she know?

No. And I haven't said anything to Dan, either. I was waiting to talk it over with you. We need to get a plan. Actually, a plot. You're good at plotting, I'd imagine. It's your profession, right? Tell me, famous novelist, what happens next?

We tackled the port. Bad idea. Akin with eating cheesecake. Lance continued to berate Dan, dredging up the times he'd supposedly power-tripped or smothered various ambitions, always to the betterment of his own interests. Snaring ownership of the farm is a typical Dan move, he said. That's how he got rich, by taking advantage of opportunity.

So this is about money?

Well, on some level, yes. Look, Amelia, you live the lifestyle of a frugal artist, good for you. But you're sitting on a mortgage-free house, on a double lot in Cabbagetown worth millions. You don't have to worry about being old and poor.

What? My little house is a wreck. And I have no intention of selling. You can carry me out of there in a pine box. It's my home. I am poor!

Yes, but you have choices, he said, his voice rising. All I've got to my name is in those suitcases upstairs.

You have a brilliant career in Vancouver. I've seen you in action. People love your cuisine.

He shook his head. Finished. I'm sick to death of the whole restaurant scene. It's hazardous to your health. After twenty years working eighteen-hour days, I've got nothing saved, no family of my own, no property. I've been in rehab twice. And I'm bored out of my mind. Moving forward, I want nothing more to do with the pseudo-art of fine cuisine, or any of the pathetic hangers-on who keep it afloat. I'd rather be a shepherd. Or fight fires. Anything. Or nothing.

What I'd really like to do is sweet fuck all. Maybe I should write a novel.

Thanks! My life's work is one rung below doing nothing?

No. It's a progression. Out of nothingness comes art.

Nice save, I said, and got up to fetch a pitcher of water. He followed me into the kitchen. I said this was pretty interesting news. I agreed to think it over. Sleep on it. I was about to head upstairs, and might well have slept on it if he hadn't insisted on emptying his cache of incendiary unknowns.

One little detail, you might want to consider …

What's that?

Well, you didn't hear this from me —

Are you sure this is something I need to know, Lance?

If you don't want to know, by all means say so.

I said I wanted to know.

Okay, Dan and Edie are on the rocks.

My legs weakened, I had to sit down on the second-to-last step. He was standing over me, hands tucked under his armpits. A fighting mode. I stood up, went upstairs. He followed me into my room. I got into bed with my clothes on, hoping he would get the message.

He said, do you want me to get you a cup of tea?

Chamomile, please.

While he was gone, I changed into pyjamas, went into the bathroom to brush my teeth, splashed my face with water, and got back into bed just as Lance was coming up the stairs with two mugs. For a second, I imagined shutting the door on him, but then I'd be left knowing the worst, when maybe hearing him out would clarify the situation and what I feared most would just dissolve.

How strange to have Lance sitting cross-legged at the foot of my four-poster. When he was little, he liked to sleep with me whenever I came home from university on weekends, a fat teddy bear between us. He'd never been attached to any particular room. He had a way of occupying every corner of the house, as if it all belonged to him. The rest of us had been insanely protective of our space. You only went into someone else's room if a major crisis was raging and had to be talked over in private — or if everybody else was definitely away, which rarely happened. In Lance's eyes, this was a major crisis, although he seemed to savour recounting the details.

Edie had been taking cooking lessons from an Italian guy who worked at the Lakeview Manor. Luigi, an actual immigrant, he was famous in Italy and extremely popular with female students. A dedicated ladies' man. Dan heard rumours and began to notice Edie was away from the house a lot, so he hired a detective to follow her. Lance didn't have details, except that Dan had enough information to convince himself Edie was having an affair.

So, he confirmed this with Edie?

Of course not! Sheesh. Can you imagine Dan ...?

My immediate response was to be furious with the two of them for prying into Edie's business and talking about it behind her back. It's not as if Dan has always been a saint, I blurted out. He had his own fling years ago, one of the interior designers working on his condo project. I was at the farm the weekend Edie found out. She came roaring up the lane right after having it out with Dan. A very bad scene, broken china, screaming, that sort of thing.

Lance was impressed. He wanted details. What did Harold think?

He pretended not to notice, went straight to bed. Edie and I stayed up all night, talking. The next day she went home, cleaned up the mess. A week or so later, Dan crawled back. That's the last I heard of it. These things tend to blow over, Lance, I think you'll find. Let's not focus on the worst-case scenario.

You could be right, Milly, but I doubt Dan has it in him to handle the situation with that kind of clarity and good sense. I tried to get him to cool down, but he insisted on digging Harold's old shotgun out of the barn. He took it with him. You should talk to him, give him some advice.

Me? Talk to Dan? Is this before or after I tell him you're suing his balls off for stealing the farm away from Harold?

Can we do that?

No! Lance, you've been back a matter of weeks, and everything is flying apart.

He leaped off the bed, began pacing back and forth on the threadbare carpet, one of the few cozy concessions in an otherwise freezing room. I was lying under a mound of blankets tucked around my throat. He didn't notice. I decided to take advantage of his emotional turmoil, make demands.

Why don't you go downstairs and pump up the thermostat, get the oil furnace going? I said. If the house is Dan's, why worry about the oil bills? Let it burn. Make Dan pay.

It isn't the money, he fumed.

Oh, okay, fossil fuels.

Nostrils flaring, hands flapping, he shouted at me: None of this is my fault. Harold jumped off the roof. We're all here right now because of him.

He didn't jump, he fell.

Impossible. What the fuck was he doing up there?

I thought Lance had heard the explanation: He was trying to adjust the satellite dish so he could watch *Downton Abbey*. At least that's what the neighbour lady who found him said. She knew him well enough to know he was a *Downton* fan.

Lance glared. He jumped to his death off the roof on purpose.

What is the basis for this ridiculous idea? Did he leave a note? No, he did not. Why would he do that?

I've been through Dad's papers. I did the math. Harold could not afford to live in the farmhouse. The upkeep sucked up every cent of his pension. His bank account and so-called investments — otherwise known as our inheritance — were long gone. He was broke. Creditors were screaming at him for payment.

Where did the money go? Did he spend it farming?

No. Well, some, probably. But most of it went to Jean and her damn charity in Africa. Dad's savings funded a series of wells and schools. Somehow, she got her hands on it, emptied his bank account too.

I pulled the covers over my head, closed my eyes. My breath reeked of port, which is not how my mouth tasted. It was bitter, like lemons, or bile. I curled up, hoping to shut out the cold and disappear into my cocoon. I heard the creak of Lance leaving the room, walking downstairs. In a few minutes, the forced air heating kicked in. He'd broken down, turned on the furnace.

My thoughts reeled back to August, the night before I left for Toronto, a dinner at Dan and Edie's. She and I took a late-night swim in their pool. Out of the blue, she started talking about Harold, how he'd been a "moral force" holding everything together. My memory contained a photographic image of the moment, her profile in the moonlight. She was smiling, her tone was wistful.

Things change, she said. Our lives won't be the same ever again.

I wondered now whether she'd been referring to herself, telling me something about her plans. That Harold's approval had been important to her. With his passing, she was free to act.

I got up, put on wool socks and a bathrobe. Lance was in the parlour dousing the coals with water when I came downstairs. The room was filling up with smoke, but he was oblivious.

Goddamm it, I've scrubbed from ceiling to basement, he sputtered. This place still reeks of tobacco smoke. It needs to be gutted, or burned to the ground.

I protested: The house smells completely different from Dad's time. It's bigger. Empty.

You grew up in a smokers' environment, he said. You're a true Catholic, Milly. You've convinced yourself everything is fine.

We all made our adjustments after a Catholic upbringing, in various ways. Lance seemed to burst onto the scene as a full-blown agnostic. He never hesitated to use his godless confidence against us. This was his Peter Pan superpower.

The old furnace made quite a roar. We stayed up for a few more minutes, until the wood smoke had dispersed or, I should say, we got used to it. In the aftermath, I thought for sure I could smell Harold's pipe, as if he'd freshly lit up and was sitting in his chair, perusing the *Picton Gazette*. I wondered if there really was such a thing as smell, or whether that, too, was an illusion mixed up with memory, tied to vague recollections of well-being or fear or disappointment. Dan claims his best Pinot Noir has floral chords of rosemary and honey, with an earthy tone in the bouquet, possibly a hint of vanilla. Nose this one, he'll say, handing over a glass. I've tried. Honestly. If you hold a glass of liquor to your nose, let the fumes drift for a minute or two, you'll be hit by a smell resembling varnish remover. This is not necessarily a flaw, it's just a fact. Somehow, we can't resist embellishing sensation with pretty words, even knowing it's largely illusion.

9

Ginny spent the holiday in Cuba with Ravi. Frank reached them on Skype before we sat down to dinner on Christmas Day. They were bronzed and glamorous, sitting around a five-star pool. When we're all together, she's just our gorgeous Ginny. To see her with her gorgeous father is to remember she is also a brown girl, her profile and poise owing much to his side of the family, his Brahmin caste, and Ivy League education. When Jean and Ravi lived in Toronto, I liked to invite them to dinner parties with, what to call it, a literary agenda? An underlying theme of networking? Ravi's an engineer but — I hate to say "but," but here it is — he reads literature and writes poetry. He was a fine addition to any lively table. Everyone loved him and hung on his conversation. Losing touch with Ravi was a painful consequence of their divorce. I tried to catch his attention around the pool, hoping Ginny's move to Montreal might reopen communication. No luck. She crushed that plan by jumping in with a question: How was my novel coming? A subject I would never have expected to be raised at a County event. I assured her all was fine. And yours?

She moved into the centre of the frame, smiling. Great! Thanks so much for your input, Aunty. Have you spoken to Barry?

I winced. Since when was she on a first-name basis with a man three times her age? My agent. She'd met him once. No, I had not been in touch.

He said he was going to call you.

Oh, yes, he left a message on my machine. I'll call him first thing in the new year.

I was mildly curious about what Barry and Ginny would have to talk about. But before I could figure out how to ask, it was Edie's turn to chat.

The next connection was with Jean in Rwanda, in a tiny village far from the capital. I hadn't seen her in ages. There she was on the laptop screen, a sturdy woman with a permanent tan, wearing an army shirt with the sleeves rolled up, looking uncannily like our mother. My first impression was she cuts her own hair, which is understandable, under the circumstances. She was sitting at a table under a corrugated roof, a half-dozen kids hanging off her elbows. The background was a somewhat bleak landscape of packed earth and skinny trees, mountains in the distance. She looked tired, as if the sun had melted her energy down to the minimum required to speak.

First, she gave a rundown on the orphanage's latest project, the installation of some kind of bio-grade well system that would produce enough fresh water for everyone within walking distance. Frank and Glenn asked a slew of technical questions. They'd been following the project for months. I stood aside, letting everybody else talk. When I moved into range of the camera, I could see myself in the tiny box at the side of the screen, a mirror image that heightened the awkwardness of the moment. A reminder to be on best behaviour.

You know, Milly, I regretted having to miss Dad's funeral, she said.

Jean always had an uncanny knack for knowing what's on my mind, especially when she doesn't approve or share my point of view.

Of course, Jean. You know what's possible and what isn't, I said.

I could have gone over, I guess, but really, what's the point? A body is nothing without the spirit. He went so quickly. Strange, though, to think of him gone, isn't it? Did you ever determine how he came to fall off the roof?

It was an accident, I said.

Yes, but what was he *doing* up there?

He was trying to adjust the satellite dish.

Dan stepped in: Jean, Dad's gone. That's the fact we're dealing with here.

She wouldn't let the moment pass.

Whatever you think. I got an odd email from Judy Wannamaker. She seemed to think that Samuelson woman was involved. Was she? What was her name? Trudy? Was there something going on between her and Dad? Judy said she was over at the farmhouse quite often the year or so before he died. She found him, right?

Dan clenched his teeth, but his voice remained even. He pointed out it was Christmas in Canada — in case she hadn't noticed. Do we need to wallow in gossip?

Lance had left the room. Out of range of the camera, Frank and Glenn laughed. Edie had slipped away and was busy in the kitchen. Jean turned the conversation to a new aid project she was working on, sponsored by an American charity. Dan asked all the right questions, including when we could expect a visit. She said she was planning to be in Toronto for a conference in late October and hoped we could all get together on the farm. Maybe we could hold a memorial for Dad? Dan picked up on the idea, promising complete co-operation. Then Jean did her usual tearful goodbye and hung up. Or whatever you call the end of a squeaky conversation on a laptop.

I find it difficult to remember — much less accurately report — any conversation with my sister. They all seem to end the same way, with all of us feeling bad, as though our lives are trivial, if not downright corrupt. I fled to the bathroom to splash my face with cold water and readjust the mask of goodwill.

Christmas dinner was lovely, memorable. Perfect, really. I was lulled into believing this year's theme would be peace on earth, goodwill to all.

10

Boxing Day, Lance had prepared supper at the farmhouse, announcing his theme as ABT: Anything But Turkey, which pleased Dan and Edie's boys. After we ate, they went off to a skating party, and Dan opened a bottle of his award-winning ice wine. He seemed edgy, kept looking down at his phone. I glanced over, noticed he was fixated on the weather page. The balmy glow of Christmas Day was gone, it was getting colder. Lance was raving about Edie's cooking, the hours she'd spent on the meal. He thanked her for helping him clean the house. And the gifts! Where do you get your energy? he asked. Are you on some kind of pep pills?

I agreed, complimented her new hairstyle. She'd always kept it long, knotted up in a roll behind. Now it was shoulder length, layered, with blond highlights. Her hair seemed to occupy more space, definitely made her look younger. I thought she'd lost weight, too, and said so. Not that she's fat, just a mother of three who loves to cook. The few extra pounds weren't noticeable until she lost them.

Edie blushed at the attention. Dan got up abruptly, headed for the kitchen with his plate and mine. Never in the history of Dan-kind has anyone seen our big brother clear the dinner table. We watched in silent awe. I noticed Dan's head go bobbing by outside, grabbed my coat, and went out. He was stalking toward the vineyard, fists clenched.

What's going on? I called out, behind his back.

Nothing. I need some air.

I had to trot to keep up. I asked him where he was going.

For a walk.

Dan, you're not wearing a coat. You'll freeze to death.

He stopped, as if the thought had not occurred to him, and looked back at the house. Then he pivoted, headed for the front door. Lance and Edie were in the kitchen, doing dishes. I followed Dan into the parlour, where he reached for the bottle of whisky on the sideboard. I was about to recommend caution when his phone rang. His side of the conversation was cryptic, full of exclamation marks and mild swearing. Hanging up, he shook his head and growled at no one in particular: temperature's sinking. Going to be forty below tonight. Bad news for the vines.

I asked if there was anything to be done about it. He ignored me, took out his phone, and started putting out calls for help.

The earth's climate is in turmoil. The night we spent trying to save Dan's precious vines from a killing frost set a twenty-year record temperature drop for one twenty-four-hour period.

Since the brutal early days of County vineyards, most growers have hilled soil over branches tied to the lower trellis wires. It's common practice, expensive, and an awful lot of work. After three consecutive mild winters, Dan hadn't bothered to hill that year. The ground remained wet until early December, so the vines had been lulled into a false sense of security. As Dan explained it, the lake has a moderating effect. The vines were at the top end of a long sloping field. If the wind dropped, the cold could potentially settle in and snuff the life out of tender canes.

I had a full range of ski clothes in Toronto but had never felt the need to bring them to the balmy County. Nor was Lance's wardrobe up to the task. So we dressed like jovial scarecrows in Dad's hodgepodge collection of woolly long johns, overcoats, hunting socks, and rubber boots.

Dan led the way, Lance and I following him to the old apple tree at the top of the field, where we would wait for the truck carrying propane stoves.

Lance started kicking around dead leaves with his foot, looking for something. Finally, he said, What happened to that boulder we used to stand on? Did you haul it away?

Dan walked a few paces, moved a dead branch that covered one side of a perfectly ordinary stone.

You're kidding. It's miniscule. That can't be it, Lance said.

We were staring at a smooth, rounded surface of grey limestone.

We used to climb onto the rock, pretend it was a ship caught in waves, vicious dragons and sharks nipping at our heels, Captain Dan shouting orders: Hold on for dear life. Jean and I shrieking like maniacs. The Dragon Game, I said. Somebody had to fall off and be rescued. It was usually Lance.

I had nightmares about dragons for years, he said.

Come on, you loved being scared and getting rescued. You used to beg us to play your game. Didn't he, Dan?

He did, Dan said. His chin was buried in a thick scarf, fur hat pulled low over his forehead. I caught his eyes, fired by moonlight, a soft look I hadn't seen in ages. A reminder of how we'd loved rescuing Lance in the endless summers of childhood. Later, we rescued him with no joy, when he fell into a dark sea of addiction, too real for our quiet tastes. Once, Dan and I had to go out to Vancouver and reclaim our little brother from his demons. But all that was behind us now, I dared to hope.

Lance turned away, picked up a frozen apple, and fired it into the night.

A contingent of helpers, mainly people who worked on the harvest, followed the truck carrying propane heaters, which Dan had found online in his early, cautious years. They knew exactly what was in store. Despite the doom in Dan's voice, a collective sense of excitement gathered as we were given our marching orders. In theory, the hot smoke would settle low on a windless night. So, we were going to warm up the entire outdoors. In addition to lighting propane heaters, we had to build dozens of small fires out of straw and wood piled along the fence lines for just such an emergency.

The propane ran out. Dan called us together to say the temperature was still dropping. We'd have to start working on Plan B: roaring bonfires of straw bales and wood at the end of the rows, which his crew had assembled while the rest of us worked. When the stoves had been gathered up and taken away, Dan doused the piles with fuel and lit them, plus a big one at the bottom of the field. The theory was that fires at the bottom would draw air movement down the slope, creating a current fed by the fires at the top. Replenishing the piles would mean a night of steady hard work.

When it was all in place, we gathered around an enormous blaze, and for the first time in hours, lowered our head coverings and looked each other in the eyes. I could tell Lance was skeptical but somehow mustered the wisdom to refrain from comment. A few minutes later Edie arrived with thermoses of coffee and shortbread cookies. As we stamped our feet and passed the mugs around, the night sky dissolved into a cold grey hue.

Through it all, Dan never stopped working, fretting. He kept walking up and down the rows, as if they were hospital beds in a war zone, peering down at his beloved vines. It occurred to me that this whole vineyard craze — at least for the sons of generational farmers — was turning out to be some kind of cruel revenge. Just when we'd been fully inoculated against one of the most difficult means of earning a living on the planet, and made other lives, along came the viticulture vogue and snatched up our eldest male. Despite his youthful rebellion against the land, Daniel Cameron was smitten. Unwittingly, he had exposed himself to the heartbreak of farming, a passion as merciless as the writing life. *We have that in common*, I thought, watching him gaze at the field. So much effort. So many ways to go wrong.

It was daylight by the time we walked back to the house in silence, single file. The air felt even colder than it had all night, though there was no way of telling whether the sensation was an accumulation or some new threshold. I was so tired I was afraid I'd keel over.

Edie had gone on ahead. As we trooped into the kitchen, we were greeted by the delicious aroma of breakfast, a generous spread of eggs, bacon, toast, and coffee. We ate like lumberjacks and laughed off the night's effort. I couldn't help thinking that this was how farmers had kept going for centuries, by facing up to the truth of the calling. In its inevitable crisis moments, working the land is never a solo act. Most often, it's a family effort.

Possibly a trick of memory, but as I think back now on that long glorious night full of fire, the pitch-black sky lit by stars watching over our peasant efforts to thwart nature, it seems like a precious moment in the history of our family. A kind of winter solstice ritual, when the distant sun stood still, then began to move back into our orbit. From now on, we would throw off familiarity and change positions, become the people we were meant to be. Not without pain, of course, but pain fades. At least the memory fades.

11

New Year's, being the passage from one year to the next, is an occasion best spent quietly, either at a small dinner party with friends or happily alone. I'd maintained this position for decades. Dan and Edie's annual New Year's Eve party was a local legend. Lance urged me to stay around, saying we had to be there for brother Dan in a stressful time, an argument I found suspect, given his revelations. Surely five days in his orbit plus one freezing all-nighter in the vineyard constituted more than enough support for whatever was ailing our brother?

An hour later, Lance mentioned he'd invited Trudy Samuelson. Did I want to meet her? Trudy Samuelson, the woman who found Harold and probably witnessed his death — a convincing reason for attending Dan's party, to be sure.

It's a rare group of adult siblings who can share friends. I stopped bringing mine to the County years ago. Separation of worlds: That's my policy. What we know about each other outside the family circle is what we've read in the papers. Over the years, I've learned quite a bit about Dan from the local press. He was president of the Chamber of Commerce. His construction company supported several amateur sports teams so he regularly turned up in the news, presenting and receiving awards. A card-carrying member of the Conservative Party, he had considerable clout behind the scenes, raising money and recruiting talent. He served on many boards. I was pretty sure his party would be a networking event. So it happened that on the afternoon of December 31, I got a ghastly haircut, spent an hour sprawled on my ancient bed, staring at the ceiling, wondering what to wear. High school revisited.

Finally, I settled on jeans and a silk blouse, until it occurred to me that Trudy might take the party seriously. So I hauled out a vintage chiffon cocktail dress, a pair of high heels, and added a significant amount of jewellery. If somebody was going to be overdressed, better the crazy aunt than a stranger invited to a clubby event for the first time.

• • •

Dan and Edie's house is a massive split-level on a two-acre lot, with a double carport, an enclosed breezeway, sunken living room, and several bathrooms. Roman grandeur, an ambitious work, never to be finished. I'd been going there for years but still didn't know my way around. They kept taking down walls, putting on additions, re-routing hallways, so there was some excuse for my continuing confusion.

A wall of windows in the living room faced the lake. On the opposite side was a gas fireplace with a marble mantle flanked by two large mirrors positioned to reflect the lake view. At the party's peak, there must have been a hundred people circulating between the kitchen, dining, and living rooms. I amused myself watching them pass — or try to pass — the mirrors. Surreptitious glances, tweaking of hair, fiddling with earrings, posture checks, tucking in of guts. Most of them eventually either turned their backs and tried not to think about their reflections, or fled to the next room.

Edie was eager to introduce her book club friends, who took it upon themselves to keep me engrossed in conversation. They'd read all of my books and wanted to hear about the next one. Eventually, I broke away and hid behind a bushy plant to wait for Trudy, although what I really wanted was to go home to bed.

Time passed slowly. I started to worry. Maybe something had happened to Lance. Maybe I'd been tricked. I noticed Dan and Edie were never in the same room together. They kept busy socializing. Dan didn't seem to need my support.

At exactly the moment I judged it was time to revisit the bar and stepped out from behind the plant, Stu Wannamaker appeared with two glasses of champagne. I looked at my watch: well past 11:00 p.m. Every time I bump into Stu I'm back in high school and just as eager to get away. Stu was in a bold mood. He'd recently bought the local Buick dealership, in addition to running what many consider the County's best garage, adding up to an awful lot of power and prestige, which he took no trouble to hide. His opening line: So you're managing to survive without your toy car?

A joke, obviously. He laughed, a derisive little chuckle that could be interpreted as insecure. Or not.

Thanks for asking, Stu. I'm thinking of buying a VW bug. Did somebody tell me you're dealing in European cars now?

No! he said, obviously horrified. But I can get you a nearly new Buick. That's the kind of car you need, Milly. Put some muscle around you. Women are better off in heavier cars, if you ask me. Better chance of survival when you crash. Ha. Ha.

I'm interested, I said, sipping the champagne he'd thrust my way. So you're finished with Toyotas? This theme carried us through a good quarter of an hour, until it was getting dangerously close to midnight. Time to duck out of kissing range. Before I could get away, he called my attention to the poisonous houseplant at our elbows, named after a great Canadian prime minister. Did I know which one? Dieffenbachia, he said, not waiting for my answer. I was about to point out that the plant predated the man from Prince Albert by several centuries, but Lance and Trudy had just entered the room. I used the excuse to wish him a quick Happy New Year and headed their way.

Trudy Samuelson's first words after Lance introduced us: You look like your feet hurt. I liked her immediately. There were no chairs left. The party was too loud for real conversation. As the midnight countdown approached, the music dropped a few decibels and the pitch of voices did too. Edie came over to chat with Trudy. Dan kept his distance.

I excused myself to find a washroom, waited for the hoopla to desist, and re-entered from another doorway across the room. Lance and Trudy were standing at the edge of the crowd, talking to each other. I took a place from which I could watch discreetly. Lance was standing close to her, leaning down, talking straight into her ear. She was nodding, laughing. A vigorous exchange: Not knowing better, I might have concluded he was trying to sell her a house, or vice versa. Then it hit me: Lance is *seeing* Trudy. This is a date.

She was not what I imagined as his type. On the short side, plumpish, with bushy red hair, somewhat older than him, she was wearing a lime-green party dress with matching shoes. She was unselfconscious, un-full of herself, unfazed by the lively mix of strangers.

I drifted, kept my eyes focused on the back of the room, hoping my stroll looked purposeful. Veering to avoid Stu, I wandered out onto the glassed-in sun porch, which was warmed for the occasion by two large space heaters. A former patio had been transformed into what they called the "summer room," meaning a three-season porch, thanks to a fierce input of hot and cold air. Dan was planning to turn it into a home office as soon as he had time to add insulation.

He was standing by himself, staring out into the yard. I came up behind him, said Happy New Year. He turned around, startled. He looked miserable.

What's up, Dan? You don't seem yourself this holiday. Missing Dad?

What? Oh. Yeah, I am, he said, sounding relieved, as though I'd stumbled on a plausible excuse for his blue mood. The yard was in darkness. He was watching the night, oblivious to our reflection in the glass. I figured his thoughts were on Edie and he couldn't think of what to say. Suddenly, he blurted out, You know what I hate about living in a small town? Everybody knows every goddamn thing about you. Nothing gets by.

Well, in a big city, nobody knows anything, unless you tell them.

I'd like that, he said. I really would.

It wouldn't last, Dan. First, you'd know nobody. Then in a year or so you'd know just as many people as you do now. That's the kind of guy you are.

True, he said, clearly taking it as a compliment. Then he turned to look straight at me. So, what did you think of that crap Jean brought up at Christmas?

That's Jean, I said. Brutal. Insensitive.

Jeez, you two are still at it after all these years. Look, Milly, let me be clear about this: I don't give a damn what Harold was up to the night he died. It's his business.

First time I'd heard him call the deceased patriarch by his proper name. I nodded. It's what people are saying that bothers me, he said.

What people?

Locals. The gossipmongers.

I don't have much connection with local mongers, I said.

We hadn't spoken about the circumstances of Harold's death since the funeral, which had not seemed like an appropriate time. In fact, there never seemed to be a good time to talk about what happened behind the accident. I could not imagine why Dan was worrying four months later, just because Jean got an email from someone she used to know in high school. Her big news could darn well stay in Rwanda. I told him so. He shook his head.

These things stick, he said.

Only if you let them. Anyway, why care? He was eighty-two, he had a good life. Maybe he drank a few shots of vodka with the neighbour woman. So what?

I'm running for mayor. That kind of shit is not helpful.

Mayor of what? I couldn't resist.

Prince Edward County! Jesus, Milly, get your head out of the clouds.

One reason I don't attend big New Year's parties is that I tend to down too many cocktails and say regrettable things. It irked me to hear him bring up the memory of our late father in the context of his political ambitions, as if the troubling circumstances of Harold's death came down to an image problem. Liquor made me more sensitive than normal. Or maybe less.

How are things with you and Edie? I shot back, thinking it was time to fight fire with fire.

He smashed one fist into the other and swore. So it's all over the place! Jesus Joseph. I'm effing ruined.

Like the good role model he aims to be, he actually self-censored the F-word.

Shhh, Dan. People read lips, you know. Family arguments at a public party are worse than rumours.

Right, yeah. He sat down on the love seat, propped up his head with one fist. I whispered, if you're seriously going into politics, for Pete's sake, learn how to keep smiling in public.

His response was a false grin. I sat down beside him. The love seat was uncomfortably full, but at least we were out of earshot.

Look, if there's anything I can do —

Talk to Edie, he murmured.

How I regretted asking.

What would I say?

Find out what the hell's going on.

Whatever's going on, Dan, I don't want to know. It's not my business.

He smirked. Come on, Lance talked. I knew he would. I don't even care. Everybody in the County knows. I want you to find out from Edie what she's up to. Make it your business. Bring me the facts.

I'm not going to spy for you, Dan.

I don't need a spy. I have one, a professional detective. Hopeless. I need to know where I stand.

Why don't you just ask her?

Are you crazy? If I so much as hint that I know what's going on, she'll kill me. Or bolt. Look, Milly, these situations are delicate. Don't be shocked, I'm going out on a limb here. (He was sweating.) If she's just … learning Italian, or whatever, well, okay, I deserve it. Revenge, I can understand. But if she's going to ditch all we've built up together for that greasy pasta pisser, then I want to know now, because I am not going down without a fight.

Why get me involved? I've never been married.

Ha! Don't play innocent, he snorted. You have a reputation for knowing what's going on at all times. Everybody confides in you … I know you know certain things. Full disclosure: I did once deviate from the straight and narrow. Edie hauled me back, and it's a damn good thing she did.

So, guilt put him in a precarious position. Outrage was spilling out of his eyeballs, but he couldn't very well play the wounded cuckold when he'd been the first to stray.

Why don't you take Edie on a vacation? (I used my best Dr. Phil voice.) Things come out when you're away from familiar territory.

That's it! He jumped up. That place in Grafton. Ste. Anne's Spa.

I could not imagine Dan at a spa, and said so.

Not me, you, he whispered. You and Edie. Go away for a couple of days, do women's stuff. She's bound to talk.

I told you, I'm not going to spy.

You don't need to spy. Just talk. If my name comes up, put in a good word. Tell her I'm ready to fight for her. I'm not going to take this sitting down. This is a matter of life and death.

Politics is a powerful drug, I thought. I said, I'm sure she'd rather hear that from you. Hoisting myself off the couch, I tried walking away but he followed.

No, no, too direct. Look, you two are close, that's a fact. I need some help here, Milly. I need to know I can count on you.

I told him the spa was insanely expensive. Edie would never believe I'd spend that kind of money on a luxury holiday forty minutes from the farm.

He agreed, said I should tell her I'd won a weekend for two in some kind of fundraising draw. Book the best rooms. I'll have my secretary phone in my credit card details.

I agreed to try, but warned him not to get his hopes up. He thanked me profusely, said he owed me a favour.

I decided to collect right away: I want you to promise me you'll get off Harold's case, okay? Let the rumours go. He's dead. He's not running for mayor. You are.

He raised an eyebrow. I kept staring at him until I got the nod.

Stu was standing by the punch bowl. I was sure he'd been watching us, wondering what we were up to. I avoided his gaze, veered into the kitchen where Frankie and Glenn were helping themselves to lasagna. Half an hour later, they drove me back to the house.

12

Adultery has never interested me as a subject for a novel, possibly because I've never been married, although transgressions of betrayal and duplicity can happen in any form of relationship. My point is, the great bombastic libidos of the twentieth century — Updike, Bellow, Amis, Mailer, Richler, Roth et al. — pretty well exhausted the subject, at least the male perspective. Sex was their religion; monogamy, a sin against the unstoppable forces of instinct and talent. Women writers of my generation tended to treat infidelity as a symptom. It's what happens if you marry the wrong person, are overcome by boredom, or discover you were meant to be something other than what you are: a housewife, mother, handmaiden. After the invention of birth control, sex replaced marriage as a stepping-stone to a woman's self-realization. Having accepted Dan's mission, I tried to locate Edie's situation inside the familiar tropes. If his suspicions turned out to be true, what was her motivation? Was she experiencing her Emma Bovary moment? She had quite a lot in common with Flaubert's heroine. Both were attractive, youngish women, married to prosperous older men of considerable social standing. They had time on their hands, a narrow range of available excitement, a lot to lose. Understandably, they could be tempted. Somehow, I doubted Edie's story would end in tragedy. I thought back to the weekend years ago, when she'd drawn me into the predicament with Dan. We didn't waste a second on the existential crisis of marriage. We treated the situation as a clear case of trespassing, an odious property infraction, and plotted the best way to pry Dan away from a harlot and get him back into the yoke of family life. We succeeded beautifully, and by outward indications he was glad we did.

This was different. Both parties were older; the boys were in their late teens, still in need of parenting yet focused on staking out independence, making plans to flee the nest. Dan found himself in an awkward position. As the first to stray, he had no right to protest. Why should I take his side if Edie simply wanted another kind of life? And yet the idea of her having an affair irked me. I felt wronged on Dan's behalf. I knew the feeling was irrational. I could not resist fighting for that marriage. I had a stake in keeping them together. I had come to rely on them as a couple, on Edie's friendship, her loyalty to my mission as a writer, her warmth and hospitality. She had a marriage I did not envy but somehow depended on. I could sit by their fire whenever I needed to and never give a second's thought to how it all worked.

As personalities, Edie and I couldn't be further apart. I'm prickly, prone to judgment; she's generous, maternal, sometimes willfully naive. After my rupture with Jean, she became my substitute sister. I admired pretty well everything about her, her grace and beauty founded on cheerfulness, her natural feminine style. When Dan first brought home a cute teenage cheerleader, I'd been skeptical, but Edie proved me wrong. The best thing I could say about my brother was that he'd had the wit to marry Edie. What on earth was she doing with an Italian lover?

I was prepared to help Dan, out of self-interest. How would I go about switching sides? With no answer to the main question, I booked us into a weekend retreat the end of January.

• • •

Ste. Anne's Spa is in the countryside, halfway between Toronto and the County exit, north of Highway 401. The original stone building is a homestead built in the mid-1800s by Samuel Massey, part of the Hart Massey clan, known for farm machinery and philanthropy. Edie was more interested in the Corcoran family, who rescued the estate from dilapidation in the early 1980s. By buying up various nearby properties, they'd created a sprawling health resort and country inn. People come from all over for the healing powers of local water and native herbs.

As the porter carried our luggage up the oak staircase to our rooms, I was glad I'd rejected Dan's idea of claiming I'd won the weekend in a contest. I said he gave it to me as an early birthday present, because I'd been having back problems following an intense period of writing. He's a generous guy who likes to roll out the red carpet. If she suspected I was building a case for my brother, she didn't let on.

Our rooms were small but smartly decorated. Measured against the gleaming decor, my clothes looked like rummage sale cast-offs, chosen with an eye for quality but well beyond their lifespan. We were issued bulky white bathrobes to be worn like monk's garb around the pool and into the various restorative procedures at our disposal. We had arrived just in time for cocktails. Edie seemed to buy the idea of Dan's gift, but I noticed she kept a bemused expression, as though she knew we were in a play and suspected there would be drama.

Dinner was a late winter menu rich in roots and preserves, prepared by the executive chef. Edie doesn't drink much; I followed her cue. We each had a glass of white wine and shared a bottle of Evian before turning in. Not a whiff of Italy on the conversational menu. Nothing I could use to pry my way into the main topic.

Over breakfast, she presented a full schedule of activities, requiring me to decide almost immediately between the contouring mudstone wrap and eight other body detox routines. Her friends had been to Ste. Anne's and recommended the stones. I didn't realize she'd already signed up for the seaweed mask when I agreed, so we spent the morning in different parts of the spa. At lunch, I was far too relaxed to focus on anything but food. Afterward, a Thai massage led directly to a nap. Edie took a walk with a woman she knew from Picton and invited her for drinks in the lobby. Fearing the friend might try wiggling her way into joining us for dinner, I tried to think of an excuse. Unnecessary. Edie whisked me away at six for a session in the hot tub, which she claimed was an excellent way to work up an appetite.

Settling into the warm water beside her, I decided it was time to seize the moment.

So, Edie, what's up with you and Luigi?

Of course I didn't start that way! If I'd had courage, or enough to drink, I might have. Instead, I floated, practiced yoga breathing techniques in an effort to quell anxiety. Finally, when the silence veered into awkward, I introduced the subject of Dan, began babbling on about how committed he was to his vineyard. What a great achievement. Who would have thought when he planted the first few rows that we'd one day be uncorking a bottle of Cameron wine at Christmas?

Dan always had drive, she said. Past tense, as though he were dead. I opened my eyes just enough to see that hers were closed. So I backed into the subject, began by saying it was none of my business. It was Dan. He's got some crazy idea that you're … well … I mean, seeing somebody else other than him. I just thought you should know. That's what he thinks.

She nodded, looked down into the water, which was opaque due to the soft lighting and dark wood finish of the walls.

Yeah, I figured he thought something like that, she said at last. Sorry. I didn't mean to …

Her voice trailed off. She kept her eyes closed, tilted her head to one side, and sighed. Steam had wilted her hair. It hung in limp wisps that just touched the water. She did not look happy. I decided to let the chasm of silence be.

Finally, she said, Look, Milly, I appreciate your concern. Really. Coming from you, it means a lot. I want you to know that Dan has nothing to worry about. Okay? I'm ready to live my own life. He'd better get used to it. But I'm not an idiot.

No! Definitely, you're not. Far from it! I wasn't implying —

I know you weren't implying anything. And I also know how much you must hate getting involved. Dan. What a jerk! He doesn't need to pester you. Why doesn't he speak for himself?

Yes! That's what I said! Well, actually, he's feeling … threatened. I guess that would be fair to say.

Is he? Ha! Nothing and no one threatens Dan Cameron. I guess he just can't believe anybody else would be interested in me.

That's not true at all. No, he definitely takes Luigi seriously.

Who?

The Italian chef. Your cooking instructor.

She laughed, not just a chuckle, an outburst that created ripples in our bath.

Dan thinks I'm having an affair with *Luigi*?

I nodded. This time her response was a derisive guffaw. Passersby turned our way to look.

Thanks for telling me, she said, sitting up straight. I can assure you I am not among the list of County women letting Mr. Pizza Dough feel them up.

She was smiling, as though I'd just offered an amusing anecdote from a planet she'd left some time ago.

Lamb was on the menu that night. I ordered a bottle of Burgundy. Edie drank two glasses and was even more cheerful than usual. We talked about her boys, their plans and quandaries about the future. Frank was about to finish his first year of engineering and was coming back to work for a local firm. Glenn had soured on the idea of architecture and was going to do sciences at York — entomology — with no firm idea about a career yet. He had a job at the Regent Theatre in Picton for the summer, showing people to their seats and getting the phone on a salary that almost covered his entertainment bills. Tommy wanted to take a year off after high school, work part-time at a hardware store. Or find work on a cruise ship and sail away, he hadn't decided. Edie hoped he'd wake up and go to university. But she doubted he could be influenced by anything she said.

As she talked, I listened carefully for Dan's interest in all of this. I told myself her concerns seemed thoroughly maternal, not those of a woman about to undertake a messy divorce. In fact she didn't seem to have any concerns that weren't common to a married woman at her stage of life. Or maybe I'm just a terrible detective.

I went to bed wondering whether I'd arrived too late to be of any help to Dan. She had said he had *nothing to worry about*, meaning Luigi was no threat. Playing back the conversation in my mind, I realized she had not confirmed that there was no one in the background. Everything about her — tone of voice, expression — seemed to shut me out. I could not bring myself to pry further. Poor Dan, he should not have engaged an emotional pacifist to act as spy.

• • •

As soon as I got back to Toronto, I called Dan, told him the news. He remained unconvinced. He said he had his sources and, anyway, Edie and I were "thick as thieves," weren't we? He probably shouldn't have hung his hopes on an expensive escapade at Ste. Anne's. He should have raised the matter with Edie himself.

Communication is always good, I said. It's never too late to talk.

He said he didn't think talk was the answer. Then he changed the subject one hundred and eighty degrees, said Lance had been pestering him about the farm, accusing him of snatching it away from Harold and doing us all out of our heritage.

You need to know that's not true at all, he said. When I was starting up the vineyard, I asked Dad to let me sever a few acres. Getting into grapes was a big investment, and I didn't want to proceed without a clear title, figuring it might lead to misunderstanding down the line. Like about now, when the vines are actually worth something. At least they were until this damn frost. Anyway, he wouldn't hear of breaking up the farm. You know, he'd rather cut off his right arm than lose a shovelful of topsoil. It was his idea to put the farm in my name.

Give you the farm, I corrected.

No, no. It wasn't like that. Milly, you jump to conclusions. He didn't *give* me the damn farm. He put my name on it.

And the difference is …? I could hear him breathing. He was not happy. I was glad not to be in the same room. He said that was exactly the kind of thing he'd expect Lance to say.

Is that why you didn't tell us?

No, I didn't tell you because Dad told me not to say anything to anybody.

Why not?

Who knows? I guess he didn't want to cause a rift.

So he left it as a surprise we could enjoy after he was dead?

I don't know. Can't you just accept that Harold Cameron had his ways? As you well know, he could be difficult. Anyway, it doesn't matter. There is no question in my mind: The farm belongs to all of us. It's our heritage, yours as well as mine, Lance's, and Jean's. So will you stop trying to churn up the past and deal with the situation in front of us?

So you're going to put our names on the deed?

A slight pause, intake of breath. Then he said, I could do that.

Well, then do it, I said.

It's going to cost an awful lot of money.

Really? Why?

Adding three more names to the title will be just like selling three quarters of the property. I'll have to pay a hefty capital gains tax bill in the hundreds of thousands. When Dad put my name on the deed, it was considered passing on a working farm to the eldest son, so pretty well tax exempt. That can't happen between siblings, and of course the farm is worth a lot more now than it was then. Technically, I mean. We aren't really thinking about selling, are we?

I didn't answer. He changed course, said he was sick of the whole thing and would be just as glad to see it all go. To be honest, I don't give a shit about it, he said. What he really wanted to do was get into politics. He was definitely running for mayor.

Good for you, I said. I'm sure you can make a valuable contribution. By the way, would you explain all of this to Lance directly? I might not be able to remember the technical details. Lance will want to know.

He promised to speak to Lance.

Only after he'd hung up did I realize I'd forgotten to ask why he'd ignored Harold's written wishes for a simple cremation and small memorial.

Once more, the facts did not exactly illuminate the problem. I was more confused than ever about the story of Harold's death or, for that matter, the quiet life I had assumed he was leading until the night he died.

PART III

Fame

13

Mid-February, Barry left a message on my answering machine requesting a meeting in his office, to be followed by lunch at a tony Queen Street West bistro. Friday, meaning the beginning of the weekend. His voice had an edge. I couldn't decide whether these omens presaged great news or the opposite, and he wanted to let me down gracefully. I'd met my October deadline in early November, but he handed it back asking for a "trim." I did my best to oblige. The final draft had arrived on his desk at the end of January, considerably shorter but still a substantial tome. I kept thinking of Shaw's famous remark, Sorry this is a long book; I didn't have time to write a short one. Unfortunately, the converse can also be true. I'd been working on this novel for several years; without a publication deadline, I couldn't find the door. Each new draft seemed fine at the moment of completion, but my own judgments never survived the necessary cooling off period. Finally, the manuscript had been yanked away from me by the Snags, for which I was grateful.

A state of gratitude is a fine place in which to meet one's agent. Barry's news was better than good. The Snag boys loved the new version. Not only were they prepared to publish, they were offering a three-book contract. He had the documents — the first sniff of paperwork I'd seen from the airport-based publishing phenomenon since learning of their virtual existence. They actually had a logo. I saw signatures in black ink, maybe not real ink, maybe virtual, but at least it looked like handwriting on a traditional contract format. I tucked the document into my purse, promising to look it over and get back to him by Monday.

A brilliant day, crisp, cloudless, we left his office in a high mood. Barry's ebullient all-business attitude was the perfect antidote to winter blues. Christmas and the aftermath had been exhausting, confusing. I dreaded the prospect of Clan Cameron falling apart, but there was little I could do. Though I sometimes ridicule his conniving antics, Barry is a brilliant strategist. I've always admired his ability to assess a situation and plot the way forward, whereas I tend to get bogged down in the complexity of hypothetical outcomes. He's a take-charge kind of guy, surely a coveted quality in an agent. As we walked along Queen Street, I considered talking over my family problems. He's been married three times. Surely a man with that much experience must have learned something.

He had reserved a corner table, which gave him a view of the entire restaurant. Barry likes to keep his back to the wall, so the guest won't be distracted from the gaze of his big blue eyes. I therefore had nowhere to look other than at him, or into a plant. He ordered the Tuscan chicken.

So, how was Tuscany? I ventured, trying to sound casual. He frowned. Didn't you get the memo? My mother wasn't well. The trip had to be postponed. Came up suddenly. I told Delores to write to everybody. Guess she assumed I'd call you myself. Sorry. Miscommunication.

I monitored my expression, concentrated on the menu, determined not to let him think I cared about being dropped from the inner circle of Tuscany guests. Poor woman, I said. How is she?

I've never gotten along with his mother. She once cornered me in her vast Italian kitchen and said I was to blame for the mess of her son's life. (*Mess*: her word.) I suggested she might look at the women he'd married. They had caused him much grief, not to mention alimony.

He might as well have married you, she said, with a deep sigh.

I looked straight at her. What an odd statement. *Might as well have married me?*

You think it's all about your damn novels, Amelia, but it isn't.

My novels have made him a lot of money, I shot back. At least *Erosion*.

Erosion! She spit out the word, said I was the "Queen of Evasion." Then she turned her back and left the room. We never again held more than a cursory conversation.

In my opinion, Henrietta Keehan is a controlling person, a greater source of trouble than any of Barry's wives. He would have been mortified to learn of her interference. He's always fretting about her well-being. His father was a famous English actor, thirty years older than Henrietta, and married when they met. From what I gathered, their relationship had been rocky, intermittent. He died when Barry was in his mid-thirties.

She's about to move into a nursing home, he said. It's going to cost a fortune, but it's her money.

In Italy?

Lord, no. Florida. She couldn't bear living in captivity with Italians. I imagine the feeling is mutual.

I mumbled something about Florida being a good choice. It's in the same time zone. She'll appreciate the weather. A sheepish observation. What I really thought was that planting his mother at the other end of the continent would be an excellent turn of events for all concerned. He said he hoped the matter would be settled soon, and the writers' gathering could resume the summer after next.

When we'd finished eating, he pulled a copy of my manuscript out of his briefcase and handed it over. I leafed through the pages, which were dotted with comments in Barry's handwriting. He's a good editor. He's literal, obsessed with accuracy and technical details, which can be frustrating, but he understands how a busy reader takes in information. His best comments are helpful; he's prepared to let go of the rest. He said it was much better, all we needed was a title.

We have a title, I said.

Really? Good. What is it?

I pointed to the title page: *Abstraction*. He laughed, said he was talking about a saleable title. I said *Abstraction* was the title I've chosen. He kept staring at the page, which was upside down. He sighed, said maybe I could give him a little background on the choice, something he could relay to the Snags, such as, what was my point?

There are moments in any creative relationship when you just have to explain your position calmly, in a definitive voice, and then say no more: Abstraction best describes the protagonist's journey. She's struggling for insight into the chaos of existence, which could ultimately only be some form of abstraction, a generalization that summed up experience and yet somehow transcended reality, but without any religious or even spiritual connotation.

As I talked, his eyes darted to the crowd behind me in the bistro, then out onto the street. During the silence that followed, I thought for sure he was going to bolt. Instead, he stroked his chin, murmured the word "abstraction," as if he'd popped a hard candy into his mouth and couldn't recognize the flavour. Eventually, his attention returned to the table, brushed past my expectant glare, and settled on the drinks menu.

Abstraction. Okay. Let's treat ourselves to a cognac, he said, signalling to the waiter.

Had he proffered an alternative title, I might have been tempted to accept it. But he didn't have a better one in mind.

So we drank the cognac and I heard more about the new company, which had evolved into SNAG Inc., standing for Stories-Novels-Alternatives-Global. They were expanding into several new "platforms" where titles could be delivered to the "story market" through a variety of ways and means. Barry had great confidence in the Snags. He predicted they would sell gazillions of books worldwide. Publishers and agents are fascinated by such details, but frankly the so-called nuts and bolts of the "industry" bore me silly. By the time a novel is handed over for publication, I'm thoroughly sick of it, usually onto the next one. The whole marketing effort feels like a distraction. I yawned. He took the hint, changed the subject.

That niece of yours is quite the talented lady, he said. I predict great things.

Really. So, you've been in touch?

She didn't tell you? She sent me a manuscript.

What?

It's good. Short, intense. To the point. She doesn't have a good title either. I'm suggesting *The World Is Your Oyster*. What do you think?

The World Is Your … I let the last word dangle. It made no sense at all.

Oyster. It's a saying.

Yes, Shakespeare. Look, I'd have to know what the novel was about before commenting on the title.

Breaking into a funny half-smile, he shrugged, said he'd presumed I already knew, and proceeded to relate the plot of

Road Trip. I barely heard. A loud brass gong pounding the walls of my head drowned out his voice.

My intention had been to correct her grammar, flesh out what she'd told me in person, and hand back a useful revision of the outline. Words just poured out. I was in some kind of fever. "The book wrote itself." Is that a plausible alibi? Afterward, I'd felt strangely relieved, exhilarated. I hadn't worked that quickly in years. Of course it occurred to me to delete the file, but I felt bad for having given Ginny mixed signals about her idea. I did not want to have a deep conversation about writing. So I sent it, with a brief note saying maybe this could be of some use. Take what you need. Make it your own. Make it your own? It *was* hers. And mine. Who knows? I did not re-read. Why hadn't she told me she'd sent it to Barry? I had a flash of Christmas, Cuba, our Skype conversation. Call Barry, she'd said. He has something to tell you. Of course.

The waiter set two espressos on the table. Barry began playing with his coffee spoon, twirling it between thumb and finger. The title could be changed, he said. Titles, who knows anything about titles, right?

The title is fine, I said.

What is it then?

Nothing, I said. Good news. So you think ... *The World Is Your Oyster* ... has possibilities?

He paused, let out a breath. So it would appear, he said. Actually, we've had an offer. He named a big-league publisher. They were starting a new line of quick fiction, thin novels with a rapid turnaround time. One of the authors in the line-up had dropped out — nervous breakdown, no manuscript — so they'd slotted in Ginny. The Canadian edition would be out in June. Instagram ads were already in progress.

June?

• • •

My head was throbbing by the time I reached home. *Road Trip* a.k.a. *Oyster* had landed a newsworthy advance from the biggest publishing house in Canada, a subsidiary of the international behemoth that had, by the way, purchased my legacy imprint after I'd been dropped from their list. In other words, this was just about the best news any author could expect to come out of the mouth of her agent.

I made a cup of tea, lay down on the sofa, and tried to sort out the situation. Not that I cared about the damn book — wait a minute! Of course I cared. Selling a first novel, any novel, is significant. As is being on the literary A-list. Dinnertime came and went. I ate nothing. Tried to watch TV. Went to bed, couldn't sleep. Took a sleeping pill, woke up feeling better. At least rested.

I phoned Ginny, told her I'd spoken to Barry, who'd relayed the news.

She said she'd wanted to call me, but Barry made her promise to let him do the talking.

Why would he do that?

Well, I don't know. He said from now on I have to let the agent do the talking, at all times.

So, he's your agent?

Yes. I mean, who else? … Do you mind?

Of course not, but —

Aunt Milly, we should put both of our names on the cover. You did so much. I mean, you *saw* the novel in the outline. You wrote it. Maybe just your name. I'm fine with that.

No. No. I did not write that novel. I don't see it that way, at all.

I was stammering, but not because I was unsure of my position. A novel comes from deep inside, I said. This one was a quick burst of writing inspired by your outline. No offence, Ginny, but it is not my kind of novel. Not what readers expect from me. You may not understand, but I do. End of conversation.

Anyway, I said, no doubt you did a lot of work on the draft I sent you.

Not really. It was pretty well perfect.

That's your opinion, Ginny.

It's Barry's opinion.

How the conversation ended is a mystery now, but I do remember staring at the phone, struggling against a powerful temptation to call Barry and fire him as my agent. For the first time, I saw clearly a truth that had eluded me for years, in fact, since the great commotion around *Erosion* that had set me on my life's work and, at the same time, had chained my talent to a rock. The man knew nothing about literature, he did not have the capacity to understand my writing, or take an interest in why I spent so many hours and gave up so much else to write what I had to write. And yet he pretended to champion my cause. Flattered me, made excuses for the steady decline in my publishing prospects, blaming the world, but all the while he was sitting across from me during hundreds of business lunches and dinners, wishing I would write another racy tear-jerker like *Erosion*. Or even better, a thin, slippery melodrama like *Road Trip*, so he could sell it to the highest bidder under a cliché title that all but 1 percent of the mass-market public would assume was totally original and mysterious. (Shakespeare! Falstaff versus Pistol: a bombastic threat of violence and thievery, but now it's considered a compliment. The world is your oyster, lucky you, young and brave.)

How many times had I noticed the season's high-brow literary tome carefully placed on his bedside table with a leather bookmark between page four and five, while beside the toilet, a leaning tower of fast-fiction with wrinkled spines, pages marred by wows and exclamation marks? He was not the high-brow literary type he pretended to be. Maybe that's too cruel. Possibly he simply did not know himself, hadn't noticed the gap between actions and words. Why did he go on representing me? I made him no money. Was it pity? Did he somehow feel better knowing he was keeping a literary charity case afloat while the halo of sensational royalties and celebrity had long since moved on? I determined to pluck up my courage and fire him at the earliest possible occasion and take the consequences. If I threw *Abstraction* to the Snags it would surely sink, and I would never know the book's true merit. Better to leave the manuscript in the desk drawer and find another line of work. At least another agent.

Had he called, or by other means attempted to contact me, I would have seized upon the opportunity and put an end to our professional relationship. But he did not. Months went by, not a word. Somehow, I could not find the right mood or even imagine the dialogue in a situation where I phoned him out of the blue or sent a letter saying … When you aren't working directly with your agent on a manuscript there is normally no need to be in touch. Eventually, a deadline would arrive and I would hear from him, or the Snags would require action. Meanwhile, my decision had been taken. I resolved to find another publisher and turned back to the task of polishing *Abstraction* with a renewed sense of purpose. I no longer felt Barry Keehan staring over my shoulder, wishing for another kind of novel. A weight had been lifted. I added fifty pages. I thought about my father.

14

By the end of March, the dirty snow had melted and some of my early bulbs were poking their heads though the topsoil. One morning I woke up to sunlight streaming through the window and a fierce longing for dear little Mini. How great it would be to jump behind the wheel and head off somewhere. I'd never thought of myself as a car person. After Mini died, taking the train had felt like a great liberation. But now the idea of calling Lance and asking to be fetched from the train station seemed too great an imposition. I wondered whether he and Dan had finally talked about the farm. Would I ever have an answer to that question unless I came right out and asked? Would it be possible, somehow, never to discuss the matter?

The girl at the car rental place was about to close by the time I turned up. I'd reserved an inexpensive compact, but she had a black SUV on the lot and offered it to me for the same price. She said it was a great highway vehicle. Climbing into the driver's seat felt like taking control of an armoured tank. After a five-minute tutorial on the various operating features, I backed out of the lot and inched along side streets back to the house, planning to leave early the next morning, after my confidence level had been restored by a good night's sleep. I thought about calling Lance, but in the end did not.

The drive was something of an ordeal, certainly not the breezy cruise I'd imagined. The tank was sturdy, powerful, nothing like the airy tin can on wheels I'd been used to. Both hands gripping the wheel, I felt small. Fragile. As if I'd somehow willed myself into a situation beyond my ability. The rental lady had set the GPS gadget on course, meaning a plummy English female voice gave fair warning as the turnoff to the County approached. If I'd had this feature last August, Mini would be alive and well today. I missed her. I missed Harold. As I pulled into the farmhouse yard, found the emergency brake, and let myself down from the heights of command, my mood was shaky. So were my legs. The side door was open. I wasn't prepared for a grand entrance.

Lance and Trudy Samuelson were sitting at the kitchen table, wearing bathrobes, eating breakfast. I looked at my watch. It was 10:00 a.m. Lance said, Well, hello, and introduced me to Trudy, who said, Don't be silly, we met at Dan's New Year's Eve party.

While Lance made a fresh pot of coffee, Trudy and I exchanged pleasantries about the weather we were having. (Sometimes I think our family missed its calling; we'd have flourished under a wartime dictatorship, where espionage is a national pastime and the ability to carry on as if nothing is amiss is key to survival.)

Lance noticed the SUV parked outside and asked if I'd bought it. Lord no, I said. A rental. I wanted to go through some of the closets, throw out the garbage, and take a few things back to Toronto. Lance said this would be the perfect time to box up Harold's old clothes for the Salvation Army. Trudy offered to help.

Just like that: The three of us had a mission.

How to describe Trudy? She had a hearty laugh, on the loud side, and piercing brown eyes that crinkled as she spoke, which was never to say anything mean or even faintly ironic. The opposite: She was unfailingly kind and tended to find everyone "lovely," but her eyes had this constant expression of mischief, which made conversation interesting. I had to work at separating words from tone of voice to figure out what she really meant.

She certainly knew how to drive a mission. By mid-afternoon we had all of Harold's personal belongings in a heap on the parlour floor. It helped, having an unemotional third party involved: Trudy suggested we extract anything that might be considered a "memento" and put it aside until the others had a chance to decide what, if anything, they wanted to keep. The clothes declared to be rags were consigned to garbage bags. The rest went into the washing machine or were neatly folded and bagged. I took the opportunity to go through my own closet, throwing out several generations of stuff I hadn't worn in years. While we worked, she brought me up to date on her own family: four boys, ages ten to twenty, no father in the picture. She lived in a rented bungalow to the east of the Cameron farm, worked as a caregiver at the Maple Manor, one of the upscale seniors' homes built on the outskirts of Picton. She liked the work although the pay was low. She adored elderly people. They have great stories to tell, although the circumstances of her work shift rarely allowed time to hear them. They were grateful, most of the time. They were often lonely. I can identify with that, she said. And yes, she was the woman who found Harold after he fell off the roof.

This bit of information she confided while Lance was out of earshot. I said I would like to hear all about it. We agreed to meet the next day, after she'd finished her shift at the Manor. In a flash, the mystery cracked open when I hadn't even been looking.

Collecting family stories is a delicate chore: One is naturally fearful of judgment, which is the *sine qua non* of narrative, otherwise all you get is plot. Until Trudy, what I knew about Harold's death and its aftermath was based on details provided by those close to me and what I personally witnessed. Faced with Trudy, I didn't feel anyone looking over my shoulder. She was honest and forthcoming to the extent that I ended up hearing more about her than the questions I had planned to ask — maybe because I found her more interesting.

This is what I came to know during the time we knew each other: She had a rough-and-tumble upbringing, her brief childhood ending when she ran away from a terrible foster home when she was fifteen, lied about her age, and got a job in a strip club. This gig went well for a few months. She concentrated on learning the ropes. One day, the boss decided she was laughing at clients as she peeled off her clothes, and he did not appreciate the joke. Ah, those mischief eyes. She seemed to view the male side of our species as a lesser model, something like domesticated animals whose welfare women are obliged to maintain. She made her life sound like a grand adventure, until she met the man of her dreams, got pregnant, got married, had her boys, and suffered their father's disappearance, which she presented as a mystery, not his fault. She swore she was not burning candles. But he was not an evil man. Your brother doesn't need to worry, she said, looking me straight in the eye: I'm as available as I've ever been. Lance is a jewel. Really, so was Harold Cameron.

Nothing Trudy said was false, yet the truth, as things turned out, was slightly to the side.

The Maple Manor was built on two acres of landscaped pasture. An unimposing low-rise, the main building is flanked by wings, creating a U-shaped interior garden with an ornate fountain so residents can sit outside in good weather and be watched from the office. The whole complex is fenced in so no one can wander off. Residents are encouraged to work in the garden, although most are not that mobile. Entering through the main door, I thought the place looked like a modest motel, minus reception. The air had a heavy, slightly sickening smell, like a combination of biscuits and disinfectant. I finally met an orderly walking by and asked after Trudy. She was in the locker room, he said. She'd be out any minute.

Our first visit after the breakfast with Lance, I had expected we would drive into Picton for a coffee, but Trudy pointed at the garden, so we sat outside with Styrofoam cups of tea, which she brought from the cafeteria. She said she'd been looking forward to meeting me. I said it bothered me that a cone of silence had descended after Harold's death. It just didn't add up, him falling off the roof.

She lowered her head, said she was constantly surprised by how twisted so-called happy families could be. They'd rather pretend to ignore a lingering fart fog than be forced to utter the word. I laughed out loud.

Trudy's account: Okay, start with me. I rented the bungalow right after we moved down here from Sudbury. I got the job at the Manor, which is where I heard about your dad, from one of the women in here. Veronica Lakey. Three-time widow, poor woman. She was a friend of his. A good friend. She was trying to get him to move in here, so they could spend more time together, but your brother Dan thought the Manor was too pricey and that Harold was capable of living on his own. Well, I'm not so sure of that. I used to drop by every few days and give him a hand cleaning up, bring over a pot of soup, that kind of thing. We'd put our feet up and shoot the breeze for an hour. He was a lovely man. Full of great stories to tell. I'm pretty sure you know them all. Anyway, like most single people his age, he was lonely. I'll tell you, he wouldn't have been had he moved in here. Men are outnumbered twenty to one. Women swarm around them like flies to honey. Jealousy is rampant. For the life of me, I do not know why. Surely after eighty they could learn to share. Anyway, your father was very fond of … well, attached to Veronica. After Dan put the kibosh on his plan to move here, he got the idea into his head she should move to the farm. I have to say, Veronica wasn't that keen on it. I guess she knew what would be expected: She'd have to cook, clean, put up with his offspring, who were none too kind — according to her. I have no idea what Harold imagined their life would be like, but he threw himself into the plan as if it was just a matter of time. He — all right, I'm not going to hold anything back — he had me send for pills. On his behalf. You know, Viagra. Well, he's a man, Milly. Men like to be involved, prepared. There's almost nothing you can't find out these days by looking on the internet. I'm not saying the little blue pills had anything to do with him falling off the roof, but Lance went wild when he found a package in the medicine cabinet. Didn't he tell you? Guess not.

So, the night of your father's death he may or may not have been on something or other. Some cocktail. Ha ha. Bad joke. He had taken to wearing the silk smoking jacket Veronica gave him one year for Christmas. And they were both watching *Downton Abbey*. It was their favourite show.

Veronica tuned in at the Manor and Harold at home. The night he fell, there was a wicked storm. The TV wasn't working properly. The roofers Dan sent over had left a ladder up against the house. I can only say your dad went up to fix the satellite dish and lost his balance. Veronica tried to phone him just as the program was over but got no answer, so she called me. I went right over. He was alive when I got there, but his body was twisted something awful. Stay still, I says, I'll call 911. No! He insisted I go inside, get a full suit of clothes and help him put them on. Well, he was wearing a flimsy paisley robe. He was mortified by the thought of Dan finding him like that. Look, I did what he asked me to. You know the awful thought? I just can't help but wonder if that poor old man would be alive today if I hadn't wasted all that time getting him into suitable clothes. Jeez. You just do your best.

She started crying. I fished around in my purse for a tissue. She took it, thanked me, blew her nose.

Veronica Lakey. Is she still living here?

She shook her head. Poor woman passed away last month. Broken-hearted.

I don't remember a thing Trudy said after that. My thoughts stayed on Veronica Lakey, a name from our past. After my mother's death, Jean and I were united in an effort to prevent newly widowed Harold from falling into the clutches of a woman we believed he met at her funeral. Well, she signed the register! We decided she was just about the worst that could happen so soon after the death of our mother from a year-long battle with cancer. Descending on a grieving man before he had time to catch a breath — we were so sure Veronica was bad news. We made a fuss until Harold agreed to stop seeing her. A year or so later, we heard she'd married someone else.

I thought of Jean, remembered she'd mentioned rumours about "that Samuelson woman" when we spoke at Christmas. Maybe she knew more than any of us. When I drifted back to the conversation, Trudy was talking about what a great storyteller Harold was, how funny he could be, and kind. Never a bad word about anybody — attributes I would not immediately have associated with my father. But what did I know about him?

I left the Manor in a state of shock, determined to head straight for Toronto. But the gas tank was near empty. I was shattered, so headed back to the farm to find Lance in the kitchen fussing over an elaborate dish involving shrimp. The dining room table was set for two.

Is Trudy coming around? I asked.

No. Did you talk to her?

He was opening a bottle of Pinot Noir, French. Yes, I said. I imagine she told you everything. Right?

Lance turned away, trying to hide a grin, but I heard it in his voice: Well, that would be hard to know, wouldn't it? I mean, what is "everything"?

Lance, you know who Veronica Lakey is, don't you?

You mean who she *was*.

The woman Dad wanted to date after Mother died. She pounced on him at the funeral! What kind of woman looks for men at funerals?

Best place to meet single men. Whatever happened to that relationship?

Jean and I nipped it in the bud. Dan took our side.

I don't remember, Lance said. Guess I was back in Vancouver.

The meal was lovely, really outstanding, from the starters to dessert. We talked about food, the County, his years in the Vancouver restaurant trade, which he now remembered with fondness. It struck me that my brother's love affair with haute cuisine was only sleeping, certainly not buried forever.

I went upstairs, stopped at Harold's bedroom, looked at the empty closet, and had a good cry thinking of the pain Jean and I — with encouragement from Dan — had foisted on an old man, in the name of what? Our own opinion of how he should behave in a time of loss? How could we have been so arrogant? So selfish? So wildly misguided and yet so confident? I had a strong urge to phone Jean, tell her everything Trudy had said, but I had no idea what time it would be in Rwanda, or whether she would even come to the phone. Veronica Lakey. All that was so long ago, our last common mission. So much had happened since. I missed the old Jean, the one who'd been so strong when our mother was dying. She would know how to soothe my desolation. She could talk me out of a massive attack of guilt, at least remind me of why we had tried so hard to save our father from himself. But I could not bring myself to call her.

• • •

My estrangement from Jean dates from long before she moved to Africa. Possibly earlier, with schoolgirl skirmishes, but in my version of events the trouble began when we were both living in Toronto in the mid-eighties. Lance was staying with me, studying to be a chef. Jean worked for a nonprofit social services agency run by our cousin, Ann Callaghan. Jean and Ann were both new to Toronto and shared an apartment. I thought they needed to meet people, dig into the city, so I invited them to gatherings and got them into splashy social events. *Erosion* had just come out, and the media attention was intense.

One night, Jean cornered me at a party and told me I'd become insufferably arrogant. If there's one quality the Camerons value above all else, it's self-effacement. We were raised to believe you don't talk about how much you earn or even acknowledge success. Any kind of fame is suspect, a trigger for certain disaster. I shrugged off her attack, put it down to too much red wine, but sensed a heavy family heritage coming down on my head. I should have acted on the clues, stepped in and reassured her it was all hype and nonsense, put her at ease. But I was wrapped up in my own world.

A few weeks later, at a film launch, Jean attracted the attention of a prominent actor. (Later she claimed I introduced them. No, he was a notorious womanizer and I would never have delivered any woman into his clutches, let alone my sister.) They started dating and for a while Jean had her own celebrity circle. A few months later, he broke it off. She was devastated. I tried to console her, went as far as spilling some rather rancid beans about his past in an attempt to reduce the pain. Big mistake. She lashed out in front of Ann and quite a few of my friends, said I was a vicious gossip for spreading lies, and she was not going to speak to me ever again. She said success had gone to my head. I was a monster.

Months passed, we didn't see each other. Meanwhile, she met Ravi, an amazing man, good-looking, well-educated, and according to Ann, thoroughly wild about Jean. It was serious from the start. Six months later they were engaged. To my great relief, Jean used the wedding to make peace and asked me to be her bridesmaid. It occurred to me she needed to flaunt her good fortune. But I was happy for her and readily agreed to spend five hundred dollars on a dress I would not wear twice.

After the wedding, she cut me off again, wouldn't return my calls. I heard she'd become depressed and quit her job. I should have contacted her, but I was afraid she would interpret my call as meddling, and it would make matters worse. Before I could figure out a plan, Ravi got a job in Calgary and they left Toronto. I heard the news only after they'd gone, from Edie, who said she was sorry I'd been in Tuscany for the going-away party on the farm. She had no idea I didn't even know they were moving. I couldn't hide my feelings, which of course made her feel bad. She tried to make excuses for why Jean had kept the news from me. We both knew none of them made sense.

The next I heard, Jean had given birth to a girl. Virginia. She was happy again. Around this time Mom got sick. We were swept up in the ordeal of her illness and death, which had the single positive side effect of bringing us closer. Jean visited often in those days. On a visit shortly after the funeral, she uncovered the budding relationship between Harold and Veronica Lakey. She was adamant he was weak and would fall into her clutches if we didn't take action. I agreed and did my best to dissuade him, visiting the farm every weekend so they had no chance to become close. Eventually, Veronica moved on to someone else. Jean was thrilled. I thought we'd patched up our differences and were once again close as sisters.

Ginny was a lovely baby, an adorable child. Everyone fell under her princess charms. For a few years, they visited the farm every summer. I made a point of joining them. The summer Ginny turned twelve, I gave her a two-piece bathing suit, pink stripes with a matching parasol. Jean was furious. She said it made her look like a tart and took it away. Ginny howled, stamped her feet, and retreated upstairs, refusing to come down for an entire day. My fault, of course. The curtain of frost descended again. They went back to Calgary. Dial tone. I was too proud, or too afraid to reach out. Edie was careful with bringing me news after that. She tried to pretend she'd been delegated messenger, but I knew that was untrue. Jean's first contract in Rwanda was for six months, then extended. Ginny stayed with Ravi in Calgary. With Jean away, I might have been able to re-establish contact with Ginny and Ravi, but I lacked confidence. I was afraid she would lash out if I tried to befriend Virginia behind her back. I didn't see my niece again until Harold's funeral.

15

The July issue of *Toronto Life* magazine ran a cover story on Fresh Fiction, identifying four new writers under the age of thirty. Virginia Gupta was on the cover, wearing a white sari, tanned and beautiful against the blue lake and a cloudless sky. Inside, a breathless personality profile presented her as an Indo-Canadian writer, voice of her generation. I was impressed by how deftly she handled the common author questions, considering she'd never actually written a book, although a relatively small part of the article concerned the book. There was scant evidence the journalist had even read it. Mostly they talked about her new boat, the MS *Alliance*, a 1987 Thundercraft Magnum 290, mint condition, 4.3 V6, 185 HP, beige and royal blue with a teak interior and a new roof. She explained how her cousins Frank, Glenn, and Tom had come to Montreal and towed her acquisition to Picton Bay, where she planned to moor for the summer while working on her creative writing thesis: a book of poetry.

"I really think a writer has to put herself in extreme situations in order to create," she was quoted as saying. As inspiration, she named her father, Ravi Gupta, who grew up in Goa and was an avid sailor, although she preferred the sturdiness of a cruiser. The MS *Alliance* slept six. She loved having friends stay overnight, it was a great party location.

I sent her a brief congratulatory email and got an instant reply inviting me to take a cruise on my next visit to the County. As if to remove all opportunity to decline, she added: We really need to talk. There's SOMETHING YOU SHOULD KNOW!!!

The sight of all caps in print scares me. I don't like visual noise — or loud punctuation. But I was pretty sure the boat trip could not be avoided. I suggested the civic holiday weekend, early August, which also happened to fall on the first anniversary of Harold's death.

Ginny had moored her prize possession in the Belleville harbour. She met me at the train station, offered to get a taxi, but I insisted on walking. It isn't every day I get to stroll down Front Street with a glamorous fashion model pulling my suitcase on wheels. She didn't seem to notice heads turning. I suppose it happens wherever she goes.

The famous MS *Alliance* was smaller than the press photos suggested. Older. I guess you would call it vintage. The deck floor was covered in a mixture of linoleum and twill rug, both quite worn. The leatherette on the driver's seat was ripped, stuffing spilled out. She gave me the full tour: Below deck was done up to look like a miniature seventies rec room, with cupboards, benches, minimalist kitchen equipment, and a laminate table that folded back to reveal a bed. The wood floors and panelled walls badly needed refinishing. All of it gave off a strong odour of motor oil. I wondered how she could sleep at night with such a smell.

Quite a few people around the harbour seemed to know her, which I took to mean she was an avid member of the nautical scene. Surely these boats underwent rigorous inspection; they must be at least as safe as a car. Despite such rational consolations, I had a queasy foreboding as she started the engine and steered the boat away from land. Her plan was to head up along the Bay of Quinte Narrows, then turn at Grassy Point, cut through Long Reach, and cruise into Picton Bay. Lance had agreed to meet us at the end of the afternoon.

I've always found it hard to enjoy manufactured events like boating, or beaches, or hobby shopping. Ginny seemed happy to motor along together. I envied her ability to just be. She was clearly at ease behind the wheel. The wind and engine noise made it difficult to talk. I was glad of the break, put my seat into recline, and leaned into thought. I may even have fallen asleep. When I next looked her way, she had turned off the motor and was setting out a picnic lunch of chicken sandwiches and cake, pouring lemonade into crystal glasses from a chilled flask.

I have a slew of gorgeous pictures from that trip, taken by Ginny. She has a talent for framing the scene. A beautiful day, I'm pictured enjoying the splash of sun and wind. We had a long conversation about the journalist who'd interviewed her for *Toronto Life*, a fine specimen of mankind. Intelligent, full of smart questions. Although he had not had time to finish reading the book when he did the interview, he'd kept in touch, asked her out to dinner. She wondered if they were dating.

Out of the blue, she brought up the subject of Barry. He's such a nice man, she said. And a great agent. She lit into a description of how much he'd done to secure publication deals, and how hard he was working alongside the publicist to be sure the book got a lot of press and sold many copies. He'd given her a thorough grounding in the perils of publishing in a digital age, when the reader's attention span is brief, legacy media crumbling by the day. She knew all about the Snags and was on a first-name basis with top figures in the business. She was enthralled by the attention of being Barry's new protegé. By the time she came up for air, my mind was somewhere else. I was looking at the shoreline, neat rows of leafy trees, rocks, familiar geography but strange, almost unreal. The Bay of Quinte and its appendages leading into Lake Ontario have been part of my mental landscape forever, yet I've spent very little time actually on the water, observing land. I was seeing a worn-out place for the first time. Barry, hovering over Ginny, conjured an equally strange scene. Overlapping worlds were not my place of comfort. I wanted her to stop talking about him, let us drift along in peace. I'd made a decision months ago but had not put it in motion. Listening to her was an unwelcome reminder of a missing scene, the one in which I would fire him as my agent. I hate secrets almost as much as I hate conflict, although there are probably plenty of both in my tangled psyche.

By the time we approached Picton Harbour it was late afternoon. A distance from the dock, she cut the motor, leaving an awkward silence. Aunt Milly, she said, remember there was something I wanted to tell you? Well, obviously I didn't get around to it. Maybe I don't even need to say it. Maybe you know. It's about *the book.* (I had no idea what was coming, though judging by her face, it was not good news.) She continued: I probably seemed like a complete idiot, the way I had an outline, but couldn't write. Okay, let's be perfectly honest: I did not write that book. You wrote it. I know you don't like it, as a novel. Which it is, I agree. But, see, to me it's, well, not fiction. I mean, I lived it. The story of *Road Trip* is my life story. At least the bit about why my parents' marriage failed, and how hard I tried to stop it, and the mess of it all. Ravi is trans. He feels female. I know it's pretty common now, but a decade ago, husbands wearing women's clothing — in Calgary — was not, well, that common. Mom couldn't handle it. She had a breakdown. That's why she moved to Africa. Sure, I changed a few details here and there, but essentially that outline is the story of my mother's, well, journey, and mine, and Dad's. I hope this doesn't upset you, the fact that I didn't mention, well, reality. Though it is kind of normal to turn real life into fiction, isn't it? Think of *Erosion*. That's basically your life story, right? Except that you had the guts to write it.

My face was numb. I simply could not move my lips, even if words had come into mind. She was looking at me, waiting for a response.

Finally, she said, You're not mad, are you?

Mad? I pictured myself mad: spikes of grey hair electrified, mouth gaping open in a Munch cry of hysteria.

No. But … how could you … not … tell me? Before I …? And then go ahead and let Barry … Your mother will kill me when she finds out her personal story is about to become public information.

My stomach heaved. I turned away, leaned over the side of the MS *Alliance*, and puked. A gust of wind blew the slur of lunch back on my blouse. Ginny shrieked, OH MY GOD! She grabbed a towel and shoved it at me. I wiped my face and clothes, murmured something inappropriate about being sorry.

I didn't mean to upset you, she said. Things just evolved that way.

Of course, now her block with the outline made sense: Putting it down had been an angry gesture aimed at hurting her parents for breaking up the family. Once it was written, she'd lost the fire, turned away. I knew this because it had happened to me. The fire from my broken heart went into *Erosion*. Once it was out, I lost connection to the past, moved on.

Oh dear, she moaned. Is this going to turn into a fiasco?

Let's hope not, I said. Start the motor. Lance is waiting for us.

He was standing on the dock, waving. Ginny waved back. When we pulled up, she paused just long enough to say hi and let me step onto the dock. Frankie and Glenn were waiting for her at a friend's cottage further up the shoreline. She disappeared before I could catch my breath.

The dock seemed to sway under my feet. I thought I might faint. Lance noticed, reached out, wrapped his arm around my shoulders, and made a joke.

What happened to you? Surely an old tugboat like this couldn't make you seasick?

He was having supper at Trudy's and invited me to join them. I begged off, blaming too much sun, so he dropped me at the house. I went straight to my room, pausing long enough to pick up a copy of the novel, which was sitting on the kitchen countertop. I had not until then actually held the book in my hands. A fiery tome, Jean's secrets spread out in print for the world to discover. So Ginny had been unable to write *her novel.* She was delighted to soak up public attention around the exposé of my sister's darkest times, knowing she would not have to wear the blame. It would only be a matter of time before Jean found out about my involvement and drew all the wrong conclusions. Once again, I would be forced to suffer the consequences of my talent for creating disorder in her life.

I stretched out on the bed, opened the first page, read a few lines, and drifted off to sleep thinking later, later, I will read this book.

16

Dan was sitting at the kitchen table when I came downstairs the next morning. He'd brought over Edie's casserole for the family dinner we were having that night, marking the first anniversary of Harold's death. He said, It seems like yesterday, doesn't it?

Yesterday. Or a hundred years ago. I would have agreed to either. How can that be? He nodded. I put on a pot of coffee.

There are times when I look at my slightly older big brother and am overcome by sympathy for his struggle to understand the world. These moments are between long stretches when his arrogance, his self-delusion and insistence on getting what he wants get on my nerves to the point where I want to slap him. This was one of the gentler times. Growing up, our father was a distant, bordering on insignificant, figure which is maybe why he loomed so large in death. Dan was my archetypal male, the one I looked up to, sought to impress, even emulate. My masculine side. I wanted to be more like him, outgoing, confident, popular. But from the time I learned to read, I was a book person, so the choice of being Dan-like was never available to me. Now, at our advanced age, I sometimes caught myself feeling sorry for my brother. He'd had no opportunity to learn introspection. Edie had taken care of emotions for both of them. He remained a simple man, perplexed by change. Now his face at repose wore evidence of pain. I had never seen him like this. I poured two cups of coffee, sat down.

He had prepared a speech: Look, Milly, I know we have to have a talk about the farm, the will, all that. God, what a year. Unbelievable. We need to involve Jean. It's hard to get her attention.

I said, She's coming in November for her memorial, isn't she? We can talk then.

Did Lance tell you about his plans to open a bed and breakfast?

Where?

Here in the house. I told him to talk to you. I'm pretty sure you'll say no.

Why would I?

Strangers … sleeping here? He shuddered.

Well, something has to be done. If a house isn't used it soon falls apart. Let's face it, Dan, this place has been falling apart since Mom died. None of us ever bothered noticing while Harold was here. He was flat broke, wasn't he? How could he have afforded to pay the bills another winter?

He shook his head. Yes, that's Lance's line of thinking. For the record, I did a lot to keep this place going. But it wasn't easy to help Dad. He considered it meddling.

I know. He had a mind of his own. Isn't that a strange thing to say? I mean, who doesn't?

He sighed. Sometimes I think I don't, I mean … really, know what to think. I'm so much better at knowing what to *do*. Except when it comes to a certain kind of situation. Then I'm …

His big hands covered his face, he rubbed his eyes.

What's the matter, Dan? This isn't about the farm, is it?

No.

What then?

When he didn't answer, I was fairly sure of what to expect. We hadn't mentioned the subject of Edie since the spa weekend in January, but the transformation in her was impossible to ignore. She'd lost a lot of weight, bought a bicycle, had her hair cut in a stylish bob, and purchased a smart wardrobe. The ten-year gap in their ages now seemed much greater. Dan, by contrast, appeared to be letting go. He was plump, grey, tired most of the time.

I had to prod. Is it Edie?

He nodded. His eyes glistened.

Oh dear. Bad news?

For me it is. I'm pretty sure she's leaving.

He folded his arms on the table and leaned on them, sobbing. My chest ached, but I could not bear the sight of his shoulders heaving. It was like witnessing nausea. I wanted him to stop. I got up and poured a tall glass of water, told him to drink it.

Sorry, he said, setting the empty glass on the table.

For God's sake, Dan, don't apologize. This is terrible. Surely you're wrong.

She's talking about getting a studio in Toronto. Why? I've been carrying this around for weeks. Feels good to get it out. What the fuck am I going to do with the rest of my life?

Whoa, let's not jump ahead, I said. It came out in a mean voice, unintended. His eyebrows shot up. The tone of reprimand worked, at least staved off another burst of tears.

Let's not make this about you, eh? What are Edie's reasons for wanting a studio? Did you ask?

He sneered, said Clive Henshaw's wife wanted "space." Two weeks after he bought her a condo in Picton some unemployed lout moved in. Turns out he'd been lurking around in the shadows Lord knows how long.

I thought back to our weekend at Ste. Anne's Spa, after which I'd reported back to Dan that there was no one else in Edie's life. Not precisely true: She'd said Dan had "nothing to worry about." What did she mean?

He looked at me. Would you talk to her?

No, Dan. I won't. I'll talk to you, because you're my brother. If Edie wants my opinion, she'll ask. Let me make one thing clear, though. Whatever happens, you will always be my brother. Edie is my friend.

That doesn't sound as good as I'd like it to sound, he said. I was counting on you as my ally.

I know nothing about marriage, and even less about divorce, I said.

That is such bullshit, Milly. You know a lot about people. Your books are full of them.

I laughed. Where did you get that idea?

I've read them.

Oh! (A disarming new image: Dan reading my books. Just this side of transgressive.) Having noticed he had my attention with that line of conversation, he pressed on.

Can't you think of a plot I could follow? What do I have to do to get through this mess? What are my options? One way or the other …

You really want to know?

Goddamm it, I do.

Suffer. You will, no matter what. In any good story, the hero suffers. In the best novels and plays, he brings it on himself.

You're blaming me for Edie's intention to trash our marriage?

I'm giving you writerly tips from my only fount of wisdom. In order to survive and regain ground, you have to give up something. What do you want most in the world right now? To keep Edie in your life?

Yes!

Well, what else?

He looked mystified. I don't know, he said. Edie takes up a lot of space in my mind these days.

You're planning to run for mayor.

Well, there's been talk. Some people think I should. Yes, I am running.

What about Edie?

What?

She wants a new life. She's a smart, energetic woman. Why not back her for mayor? Throw your support her way, become her campaign manager. I'm sure with your clout and connections you can bring your supporters onside. You'll be able to finance the campaign and groom her for the job. Dan, she's served on so many committees and accomplished a lot for local causes. Edie would be an excellent mayor of Prince Edward County. There aren't enough women in politics. How many times have you heard that? Her job as mother is winding down now that the boys are leaving home. From what I can see, she's terrified about turning into an idle housewife. She needs a new challenge. This could be it.

He shook his head, said Lance was counting on her to help run the B&B.

Really? That is a pathetic excuse, not to mention a very bad idea. It's only going to institutionalize and perpetuate the skills she invested in motherhood. Edie in the kitchen? That won't be enough. And will it really work for you?

He looked around the room with new eyes, imagining Edie preparing delicious food for strangers. A terrifying scene.

I thought it best to prepare him: Don't assume she'll say yes.

No. But. Yes. Mayor? I guess it's worth a try. I'll ask her.

17

On September 4, I opened *The Globe and Mail* and found a news item that blew my proverbial socks off. *The World Is Your Oyster* was on the Giller Prize long list, Canadian literature's brass ring. In addition to a six-figure cheque presented to the author at a televised gala, the winning book would enjoy scads of promotion, a guaranteed boost in sales, and a permanent place in literary history. The list of laureates is a who's who of Canadian fiction.

While I still held the pages in my hands, the phone rang. It was Ginny, wondering if I'd heard the news.

Indeed.

A pause, during which I tried to think of something casual, wise, or even jocular to say. Nothing came to mind.

She broke the silence. Aunt Milly? Hello?

Ginny, congratulations.

What do you mean? What about us?

The sound of water splashing. Her voice muffled, far away.

Where are you?

I'm on the MS *Alliance*, anchored right across from the farm. This is kind of wild, don't you think? I mean, I never … I didn't think *Oyster* was *that* good. Well-written, sure, but wow!

I reminded her it was only the long list.

She gushed: Barry thinks *Oyster*'s got a good chance at winning. He says it's a fresh story. Juries like new voices. He's going after a film deal. Sarah Polley's reading it right now. Wouldn't that be amazing? I'm definitely up for writing the screenplay. You know, my undergrad degree was in film studies. Isn't that ironic? Maybe I'm meant to be a screenwriter. I love writing dialogue and material with lots of locations. I can see myself in the film industry even more than literature. But that can wait. When do you think we should tell the media about your involvement? … Are you there? … Is something wrong?

No, no. I'm just surprised. Ginny, don't say anything about my … about me. Keep my name out of this. I want you to promise.

She moaned. Oh. This is … awkward. I hope you're not blaming me, because it's not my fault. You didn't want your name on the cover. I was only … I wish you'd say something!

I was numb. I could hear her breathing intensify.

Maybe I should call Barry, get his advice, she said.

No, don't do that.

Why not?

He wouldn't understand.

The prospect of *Oyster* winning a major award was disorienting, but I did not need to consult Barry in order to gauge his opinion. He certainly would forbid us to go public with the co-authorship. Controversy of any sort would put the jury off. And a book by a fresh, young, semi-Indian authoress was far more likely to win than one co-authored with an aging has-been. A mental image of Barry's furrowed brow clarified the situation. That's how well I know him. I had to find a way to explain, without explaining.

Ginny, listen carefully. It's the book that's up for a prize, not the writer. And it is your story. You took the decision to show the manuscript to my agent because you believed in it, so let's stay with that decision. When *Oyster* does — or doesn't — win, we can talk again. All right? In the meantime, say nothing about any personal aspect of the novel. Do you understand?

I guess so, she said, sounding less than convinced.

Including the part about your parents.

Oh yeah, right.

I was tempted to ask if they'd read the novel, but resisted.

She said she was nervous about all the publicity. What should she say?

Just carry on as you did in *Toronto Life*, I said. You were charming.

You think so, really? Thanks.

Yes. Congratulations. Goodbye, Ginny.

• • •

A few hours later, Barry called. His voice was warm and fuzzy, as if we were about to pick up a cheerful conversation dropped a few days ago. I made it easy for him, said I'd heard about the nomination and had already phoned Ginny with congratulations.

A nervous laugh, then he said, These damn contests are a lottery, aren't they? Doesn't mean much in the long run, as I'm sure you'd be the first to say. Anyway, you need to come into the office. Is today convenient? Five p.m.?

We hadn't spoken in months, and now he was summoning me.

As Delores ushered me into the inner sanctum, he was at his desk, on the phone, looking out the window. I sat down on the sofa. While he made a show of trying to wind down the call, Delores entered with a tray bearing a cold bottle of Perrier, two crystal glasses, and a small bowl containing a healthy mixture of nuts and dried fruit. After she set it on the coffee table, I selected a cranberry and leaned back on an ample cushion. The call over, Barry turned his phone off and sat on the sofa across from me. He poured himself a glass of Perrier. I noticed his hand was shaking. I asked if he was feeling all right.

He said he'd never felt better.

He had definitely looked better. His face was flushed. He was on the verge of speaking, but said nothing. Finally,

I asked outright, What is the purpose of the meeting? He got up, strode over to his desk and retrieved a cardboard box from behind the chair, took out two books, and brought them over to me. The cover was matte white, the type a shiny black raised font. Sober. Impressive. It looked seriously important. The font on the back was big, bold, bursting with accolades from fellow writers.

ABSTRACTION
a novel by Amelia Cameron

He was hovering, waiting for a reaction. I looked up at him. He stared at the floor, his face set in a defensive grimace.

Opening the cover, I looked at the first page. Blank. Second page, blank, and so on until, finally, print. At the top of the page, a number; top of the next page, another number. And underneath the numbers, letters, words, sentences. Upside down. I kept turning, stopped and looked over at him. His arms were crossed.

Arriving at the last page, I noticed it was the first page of the novel. I turned it over, started from the other end. This time the text made sense — elegant font, wide margins. But now the cover was upside down.

They printed my book upside down?

Not necessarily, he said, looking down at his Italian-made shoes. I ran over to his desk, started taking books out of the box. Twenty copies, identically misprinted.

I snapped. What the hell is going on? This is a terrible mistake!

Somebody in Delhi screwed up, he said, getting up. You can imagine how hard it is to communicate —

Tell me you're going to make them reprint.

It's not that simple, he said. There's a question of time, and the cost —

I threw a book at him, catching him on the shoulder. He ducked the second and third copies, raised his arms against the blizzard, but I kept on until the box was empty.

How can you expect me to accept this travesty?

He grabbed my hand as I reached for a tiny Inuit sculpture on his desk.

Wait, I can explain, he said.

I don't want an explanation! I want a correction.

You can't correct —

Reprint!

He leaned forward, grabbed me in a bear hug. A bold move, he meant well, but it didn't work. I felt like a straightjacket was on the way, wiggled out of his grasp, and stepped back.

Amelia, please. It was a mistake, he pleaded. I'll grant you that. Riki called from Frankfurt.

Who is Riki?

One of the Snags.

Riki felt terrible about the cover. He was prepared to reprint, but reprinting in India takes time. They have a wide-ranging virtual campaign gearing up. They needed to get product out in order to take advantage of the splash, so to speak. They're revved up, ready to launch. Anyway, we can't let a last century's artifact stand in the way of success. It's the ebook that counts.

What? Last century's — So the real book isn't important?

Of course it is, we have to have a "book." They'll definitely want to correct it for the second edition. On demand. Surely you've heard of print-on-demand.

Yes, I have! I demand a reprint!

In due time. Look, given the themes of your novel, I think we can pull this off. There is a connection. Maybe even an up-side. Value added.

What?

They're sending out a press release drawing attention to the innovation.

Innovation?

It's basically a gimmick. Black type on white cover is a distinguishing feature, but it's not original. Whereas cover text upside down is bold. Practically an abstraction. Get it? And we've secured front table space at Indigo. Fifty copies one way, fifty the other, plus window displays. Pretty impressive, I'd say. These days only potential bestsellers can motivate a big-chain bookstore offer of storefront displays.

Downtown?

He nodded. And many, many malls. Isn't that great?

I picked up a copy of the book. The cover had been creased in the storm. I tossed it back into the box and told him I had to get to another appointment. I was late. On my way out, I looked him straight in the eye and said that under no circumstances would I permit the launch of a damaged book. Reprint, and then we launch. Tell the Snags this is an unsurmountable snag.

Delores was bent over her computer screen and appeared not to notice as I rushed past her desk.

18

The Giller short list was announced in early October. *The World Is Your Oyster* made it. Virginia Gupta put her academic commitments on hold to embrace her new role as media star. You couldn't open a newspaper or magazine without seeing her face. Often there was water in the background. She did the talk show circuit, gave her opinion on all manner of topical issues. She turned up on TV wearing a sari for a discussion of ethnicity and celebrity. She claimed to be well into her second novel, which was set in Goa.

I left her a voice message but she didn't return the call. The author was too busy to visit the farm. Frank kept in touch. He said she sometimes bunked with friends in a Queen Street loft but was spending a lot of time on her boat, now docked off Toronto Island.

Edie and Lance followed the hype. They'd read the book and proclaimed it very good for a first novel, lively, funny, outrageous. Their praise straddled a fine line of familial loyalty, including hints that it wasn't as deep or as important as my books, but a hell of a good read just the same. In other words, a prizewinner. A bestseller. The kind of book I wouldn't bother to write. I pretended to be enthusiastic about *Oyster*, but the effort came across as a pathetic form of jealousy, made worse by Edie's polite questions about my novel-in-progress. Yes, *Abstraction* was coming out soon, I assured the table. There would be publicity of some sort, but it was too late for this year's prizes.

To say that I didn't care about prizes would have sounded like a dismissal of Ginny's success. So I had to care. And yet not care. It was all immensely awkward. On the positive side, no one talked about the farm. I appreciated the gesture from Lance, who was obviously burning to discuss his favourite subject. Meanwhile, I had landed a contract editing a technical manual, easy work that paid a few bills and helped keep my mind off the subject of books.

At least until the night one of my oldest friends, Jacques Durand, invited me to a dinner party. A professor of French literature, Jacques has a doctorate from the Sorbonne, a heavy French accent, and a large following of female admirers. He also has his fingers in many pies; he runs a popular website that publishes reviews and insider gossip. His ability to gather information and drop it into the common pool at strategic moments is formidable. People with books to sell seek him out or hide from him in equal measure. He's consummately friendly and can also be dangerous.

The subject of the night was the Giller. To be expected, Jacques knew people on the jury. His dinner guests were players on the literary scene. They may have had opinions on the artistic merit of nominees, but that night all they talked about was the odds on who would win. They had good arguments for all five candidates. I tried to stay in the conversation by making innocuous comments following other guests' opinions, without actually favouring a particular book. Toward the end of a long arc of debate, Jacques turned the attention on me by asking point-blank who I thought should win.

Well, *should* win? That's a complicated question. We all have different tastes. The five books have merit.

Yes, of course. But do you have a personal favourite?

I'm sure I blushed. Everybody laughed.

You see, we're being unfair. Playing with you, my dear. Of course we know Virginia Gupta is your niece. You're bound to favour the family, *non*?

Flashing back over the conversation up to this point, I tried to process how many times I'd said something ridiculous to people who knew more than I thought they knew. So, I was trapped in a remake of the famous French comedy, *Le dîner de cons*. I was the idiot brought in for the amusement of smarter guests.

I decided to aim for the high road. To be honest, I haven't read it. I'm familiar with an early draft, but this has been Ginny's baby from the start. Surely you can't expect me to be objective.

He refused to concede: Why did you keep your relationship a secret?

The table was focused on me. For once, I paused to consider what was on the tip of my tongue, and swallowed it. Then I spoke.

I didn't want to steal her limelight. She's so young and – you know how the young are — they believe they've invented the world.

But she's following in your footsteps, Jacques said. Surely there's an influence.

Possibly, but I'm not in a position to say.

This prompted another guest, an influential critic, to opine about the similarities between *Erosion* and *Oyster*: explosive plot, fast pace, lyrical prose, tight structure.

My head throbbed. I said I was sorry, but I couldn't be objective.

Perfectly normal, Jacques declared. In time you will, or at least the critics will put the pieces together.

Everybody laughed, and the conversation moved on. Gossip mostly. Excruciating. I thought the evening would never end.

Finally, the party's dominant female stood up to leave, prompting a stampede for the door. Jacques touched my hand and whispered, Stay for a nightcap. I have something for you.

Years ago, Jacques and I had been involved, briefly. He's a charmer, a free-floating, always available natural resource — of late, an endangered species. I started clearing the table but he wouldn't hear of it. He cranked up the gas fireplace and produced a spectacular bottle of Gigondas, which he had uncorked hours ago in anticipation of the moment. It was a relief to be out of the hot seat. I thought I'd played the evening quite well, all things considered. I was clear-headed, drank one glass of wine, and hadn't said anything worthy of regret.

When we'd settled in and he'd treated me to some tasty gossip about the departed guests, I asked him what he'd been planning to tell me. He laughed.

Well, I must appreciate your Canadian directness, *non*?

That's up to you, I said.

All right. Let me try being Canadian. I think *The World Is Your Oyster* is your oyster.

What?

You wrote the book.

No!

Voyons, Amelia. We have known each other for many years. You can be honest with me.

I said I didn't see the slightest connection between those two statements.

He laughed. So you wrote it but you don't want to tell me? He gave one of his famous Gallic shrugs.

You have to admire a culture so loyal to its clichés, although this one is so eloquent and useful it deserves to endure. Thinking back over the evening, I realized everyone at the dinner thought I'd written *Oyster*. It was Jacques's mission to authenticate their hunch. To be honest, the whole game pleased me. For one brief moment, I had exactly the kind of fame I like: secret admiration, without the awful responsibility of ownership. This perverse relationship with the art form defines me as a writer, maybe as a person. I don't care what everybody thinks, only a select few. These were my peers, and they knew my secret. I could write popular books, but I don't. What could be more delicious? Furthermore, I was sure Jacques understood perfectly, and approved, which is why, perversely, he would agree to tell no one, and be sure to tell everyone.

Ah yes, he said, with a crooked smile, index and thumb stroking his little grey beard. You know, it's an old story. The family genius. Surely you've heard about the French author Romain Gary, who wrote France's most popular twentieth-century novel under a pseudonym and thereby won his second Prix Goncourt? A prestigious award, it is given only once to an author.

I had a vague recollection of the story, but Jacques knew all the shadowy corners.

A prolific, multi-talented immigrant, Gary won the Goncourt in 1956, but by the seventies he'd fallen out of fashion. So he concocted a new identity — Émile Ajar, a young Franco-Algerian medical student exiled in Brazil. When the second Ajar novel attracted serious acclaim, Gary had to produce a body to defend it, so he convinced his distant cousin, Paul Pavlowitch, to play the part. *La Vie devant soi*, a heart-rending tale about an Arab boy living with his Jewish foster mother, touched on all the French tropes of the century and won the Goncourt in 1975. "Ajar" a.k.a. Pavlowitch, became a public personality. The critics raised him to the pantheon of important writers.

On that note, he refilled our glasses and sat back.

Well, how did it end? I tried not to sound desperate.

Ah! My dear Amelia! Can you imagine such a story ending well? Five years later, Gary — who had a stormy love life — shot himself. He left a suicide note in which he revealed the truth about Ajar. Of course he laughed at the French establishment, who had been so easily fooled. As you must be laughing, *chérie*.

And what happened to the cousin?

For many years he lived in the shadows. I believe, yes, he published a few novels while living somewhere in a small village … No one follows him.

A terrible wave washed over me, the same feeling I'd had on Ginny's boat when she confessed the outline was truth, her mother's meltdown. Yes, I would get insider credit for writing *Oyster*, but if the book became truly famous, Jean would suffer widespread lasting exposure of the most painful loss of her life: the loss of Ravi, her wonderful man — a deafening echo of the pain she'd felt when her relationship with a famous actor fell apart. I would be blamed.

I had one chance to dampen the flames. I took it, asked him to speak to someone on the jury, tell them about the muddy authorship. It's a small world, I said. Your dinner guests know the truth. How long before word gets around? We can't let a prestigious literary award be tainted by scandal.

The Giller is too important to Canadian literature. I don't want to cause a scandal. These institutions are always fragile.

He said he admired my altruism. Very few authors would let such an opportunity slip by. I thanked him but assured him there was a strong element of self-interest involved. I had another book ready for press, a novel I was ready to own. I didn't need controversy to muddy the water.

19

The Giller Prize didn't exist when *Erosion* came out. In those days, the ticket to success was getting a spate of good reviews from famous critics, which led to catchy blurbs on the paperback edition, general media coverage and vigorous sales, maybe a film. Writing novels wasn't yet a gladiator sport, with winners and losers. If you published a novel, you were a winner. I've won a few literary prizes, but never thought of myself as working in the jungle of commercial fiction. I suppose if I'd paid attention to the popular press, I would have known that in this new century "literary fiction" has ceased to occupy the status it enjoyed at the invention of CanLit. The greats from the past retain their iconic "brands," but as for living writers, few people outside academe talk about the "body of work." The term itself may have been invented by Barry, in order to classify me beyond the reach of disappointment.

Two days before the gala ceremony, a splashy televised event, Barry called. He said we needed to talk. Could I meet him somewhere? I suggested his office.

Not here, he said, in a low voice, as if someone might be listening.

I named a few public places. None were acceptable. Finally, he said he'd prefer to come to my house. By then his telephone voice had broken down into a nervous stammer. I couldn't imagine what was on his mind. Maybe the Snags had crashed, and all copies of my desperate novel were on their way to the paper shredder. From the beginning, I'd had no confidence in that scheme.

Half an hour later, he appeared at the door carrying a large cardboard box. Face flushed, he staggered past me and went into the kitchen.

Your books. Ouch, my back.

I pointed at the door: On the curb, please. Tomorrow is recycling day.

He deposited the box on the table and headed back out to his car. I followed, warned him not to bring more of the misprinted upside-down covers into my house.

They're garbage. I'm expecting a reprint.

Fine, but that's not why I'm here, he said, turning back. I need a drink.

He winced at the offer of tea or coffee, reluctantly chose tea, and went into the living room. When I emerged from the kitchen with a tray, he had settled into his favourite chair, a wide floral number that had been pretty well destroyed by my last dog, a mongrel hound who died of old age. I had intended to throw it out but hadn't got around to it. We made small talk about the dog. Barry thought the chair should be reupholstered, in memory of the deceased. He offered to contribute. I told him to get to the point. He made a great show of stirring milk and sugar into his cup. During all the years we've known each other, I have never seen Barry touch tea. He still hadn't raised the cup to his lips when he said, It's about Ginny.

What about her?

She … hmm. How to put this? She's disappeared.

What? How do you know?

The publisher can't find her. She's not returning calls. This is serious. Ginny has to be present at the gala. When did you last hear from her?

I hadn't seen her since the civic holiday weekend, the boat trip. We'd talked about getting together but she was too busy publicizing the book. She's a bit scattered, I said, but surely she will reappear in time for the big event. Probably at the last minute.

He got up, dumped his tea into the kitchen sink, and came out with two glasses. I produced a bottle of single malt and poured us each a generous shot.

The thing is, he said, after gulping it down, she's probably on one of those first-time author meltdowns, nothing to be worried about. Could even be good. I mean, a stunt. Ultimately. But I need a Plan B. I can't show up at the Giller without an author, in case we win. Which I think we will.

I could have put his mind at ease by assuring him there was zero chance of *Oyster* winning the Giller. Jacques Durand had promised to save our souls, for the good of the award and my family life. But if I told him the truth, Barry would have had a heart attack on my carpet. Instead, I refilled his glass and advised him to sit down. Calm down.

He took my advice. Then he said he had a Plan B, and pointed at me.

I want you to come to the award ceremony with me, he said.

Out of the question. I have plans.

What? You're watching it on TV?

No. If you must know, I'm going to concentrate on finding my niece.

Don't worry about Ginny. Look, to put your mind at ease, she did drop me a few strong hints along the way. She said she dreaded the event. It should be you up there.

Why?

You tell me.

He was now deeply ensconced in the old dog's chair. His stress level upon entering my house appeared to have dropped considerably. Surely it wasn't just the liquor. He clearly had more to say. I considered waiting until he created a believable narrative around his visit, but there was no point in being subtle.

Barry, I sense you are holding back. What have you come here to say?

I would like you to go with me to the Giller awards. Please.

I have nothing to wear.

He got up, went out to his car, and came back with a box from Holt Renfrew. Inside was a floor-length, raven-black silk gown, with a ferocious amount of beadwork sewn into the neckline. In another box, an accent bag and matching shoes.

Where did you get all this?

Holt Renfrew, he said. Try it on.

What? When?

Right now.

No, I mean when did you buy this outfit?

Today. I figured you'd say you had nothing to wear. And the event is tomorrow night. Amelia, please do me this one small favour. I haven't had an author at the Giller in eons. Win or lose, I need to be there, meet people, be seen. After all, you are the author's aunt. People will expect you're an influence. What a story: Amelia Cameron's Niece Wins Giller Prize. Look, these days we can't afford to pass up a single iota of attention. Who knows when the opportunity will come around again? We aren't getting any younger, you know. Every millennial with ten fingers is writing a fucking novel. The rest are using Dictaphones. Don't quote me.

I laughed. Then I said, Barry, I am seriously worried about Ginny. This isn't like her.

Oh, it is like her, he said, lowering head. Trust me, I know Ginny.

I did not like the tone of his voice. It left room for a level of intimacy that I did not find acceptable. And yet, what right did I have to protest? Above all else, I did not want Barry to think I cared if he was smitten by my niece. So I said, Okay, I'll go. For Virginia's sake.

The dress fit perfectly, so did the shoes. Stranger still, it all looked quite wonderful. I managed to book a hairdresser and have my nails done. A *Vogue* cover look, if I do say so. Barry wore his tuxedo. He usually drives an ancient, messy, low-slung MGB, which he claims is a vintage jewel, but he'd hired a limo for the occasion. As he opened the door to the back seat, he brushed off the luxury, saying there was so much good liquor ahead, he didn't want to be a designated driver. I said I could have driven, I'm not much of a drinker.

You're not much of a driver, he said.

Everybody was there: the Toronto literary mafia, the millionaires, acolytes, aficionados, and celebrities eager to turn a small flame of glory into a capital-sized bonfire. A few minutes into the cocktails, I spotted Jacques Durand on the arm of a fresh-faced poet who had been his student, if memory served. He sidled over, winked and wished me luck. I thanked him, sincerely. People I knew and some I didn't kept coming over to chat. I wondered if Jacques had declared a total dis-embargo on the information we discussed. For the aunt of a nominee, I was paid an awful lot of attention. Or maybe it was my imagination.

The prize went to an eight-hundred-page historical thriller set in an Inuit village at the turn of the century, the first novel of a hitherto unknown writer in her late fifties. I went out and bought a copy the next day. It's good, unusual, a story that needed to be told. But then I have a weakness for ambitious, discursive narratives by authors with the courage to believe readers will turn pages without the enticement of a murder to be solved.

Barry was disappointed. He swore the draw was fixed. He'd been looking forward to managing success, cashing in on soaring royalties, selling world rights. His mood perked up considerably when he spied the legendary Anita Brooks coming our way. The senior editor at my old publishing house, now head of a prestigious literary imprint, she's someone I often saw socially in the glory days of *Erosion*. Our paths diverged when I moved down the ladder. She greeted me like an old friend, kisses on both cheeks, actually took me by the elbow and leaned in to whisper — loudly — Amelia, you've got to promise me a first look at your next novel. Will you do that?

I'm fairly certain she emphasized the word *next*. Then she winked at Barry, saying, Unless your agent has other plans.

Barry assured her she would be given a first look at the work-in-progress.

It was well after midnight by the time we got back to my house. The limo had been an arrival prop. We took a cab home, which he sent away before I reached the door. Just a quick nightcap, he said, and promised not to stay more than half an hour.

I went into the kitchen to put on the teakettle. He followed.

As we were waiting, I thanked him for the evening, said I thought it was a fine ending to our run as author and agent. I appreciated his years of effort on behalf of my work. Of course we could still be friends, but my writing would no longer be a subject for discussion between us.

He nodded, stared at the floor, said he understood. I thought, *How could that possibly be true*? You haven't even bothered to ask me why I'm firing you.

Then he said, There's something I have to tell you. It concerns Ginny.

He paused long enough for me to catch my breath.

She flew out to Rwanda yesterday. Her mother's not well. She's going to stay there for a while until Jean is able to travel.

What?

Malaria. Bad attack. Look, it was Ginny's idea that you go to the award ceremony and represent the book, in case we won.

Why didn't you tell me?

I'm selfish. I wanted to be there with you, without fretting all night about things nobody can control. I wanted you to have fun. Did you?

Fun?

He said, Oh God, and hung his head.

I tried to reach Jean by phone, then on Skype, couldn't get a connection. I called Edie, woke her up. She said Ginny had sent an email. Her mother was receiving medical care and would soon be able to leave for a hospital in Kigali. They would fly to Toronto as soon as Jean felt well enough. She'd call if anything else came through.

Barry insisted on staying around while I made the calls. It was 3:00 a.m. by the time I finally calmed down. He had polished off the malt and was in no position to leave the building, maybe not even the chair.

As I handed him a fuzzy throw and an extra pillow, he leaned forward and took my hand.

I just want to say how sorry I am to have withheld bad news until after the ceremony. The truth is, my feelings about you are so mixed up, I lose sight of ...

I said he shouldn't worry. He'd had a lot to drink and we were both tired.

I was tempted to offer him the other side of my bed. From time to time, something happens that throws us back into intimacy. The next morning life goes on, as if nothing happened. I really don't understand, neither does he. This time, I was too churned up to risk repeating the eternal mystery. So I said I hoped the sofa would be comfortable and got out an extra blanket.

It took me ages to fall asleep. I thought I could hear him talking on his cellphone in a low voice, but when I went to the top of the stairs to check, he was still sitting in the old dog's chair, staring into the dark.

PART IV

Fortune

20

Sister Jean, our Mother Teresa, our moral compass, guardian of our social conscience — her visits from Africa always leave me feeling personally responsible for the ravages of capitalism. I deeply admire her commitment to the suffering world and have contributed as much as I could afford to the cause. But facing Jean in person, I tremble. Dan feels the same way. He once hid a new Mercedes in the barn rather than risk a withering look from the One Who Cares. The idea that she might actually be dying was unfathomable.

After three days with no news, Ginny sent Edie an email saying they'd made it to Amsterdam and would board a plane for Toronto the next day. Lance called to say he was borrowing Dan's SUV and would meet them at the airport. They probably had a lot of luggage. Did I want him to swing by and pick me up? I was surprised to hear Jean wasn't staying in Toronto for medical attention, but Lance said her condition had stabilized. She was anxious to start working on the memorial for Dad as soon as she arrived.

Really? She collapses with malaria and then plunges straight into organizing a memorial service in the County? In addition to travelling with a halo over her head, our middle sister has a taste for drama that seems downright un-Cameron.

Hey, I'm only following orders, Lance said. Let's see how she looks, take it from there.

When I phoned Barry to let him know his client would soon be back in town, he insisted on driving me to the airport to meet them. We were there half an hour before the 11:00 a.m. arrival. Lance was nowhere to be seen. As a motley band of sleepy passengers began streaming through the doors, I was overcome by a feeling that Jean would not be among them. A woman in her condition would surely have priority. My heart was pounding. Finally, among the last to disembark: Ginny pushing a wheelchair bearing a shrunken woman who hardly resembled the person I knew. Her hair was grey, thin as cobwebs. She'd lost a lot of weight. Her skin was loose, transparent. I stood motionless as the cortège approached. Her eyes seemed huge, her gaze passing straight through me.

Lance appeared from the crowd and stepped forward to take Ginny's carry-on bag. Jean nodded at me and mouthed my name. I started to cry. Ginny gave me a big bear hug, then turned and hugged Barry.

They had an enormous amount of luggage, which just left room for two passengers in the SUV, so Ginny offered to ride with Barry. I helped Jean into the van beside Lance and got in the back seat. Barry came over and motioned I should roll down the window.

Are you all right? You're not too squeezed in?

I said I was fine. There might actually be room for Ginny. Save you the bother of driving all the way to the County.

It's no bother at all, he said. But maybe Ginny would rather ride with her mother? You could come with me.

After twenty-two hours in the air she'd probably rather talk to her agent, I said. He laughed, said he'd see me at the farm.

Barry thrives in a crisis. He's an active member of PEN International, a master at getting oppressed writers out of sticky situations in war-torn countries. I sometimes wonder why he stayed with the literary crowd so long. We're a morose lot, solitary, difficult to help, and so rarely satisfied.

As we drove out of the airport maze Jean withdrew, her shoulders slumped. I tried to see what she saw: dense apartment towers, warehouses, and monster hotels clinging to the outskirts of the city. Then bare wintery trees, grey fields bereft of snow, a tight string of gas-guzzling cars and trucks shooting past. For years I'd read her gaze as critical, but now I wasn't sure. Her gaunt eyes seemed to devour the landscape, the way a starving person might regard nourishment, or a sleeper gaze at a dreamscape she knows is unreal yet somehow believes in. She wasn't sad or hostile. She exuded a quiet, childlike joy. At one point, she turned to me and asked what day it was. Saturday, I said. She nodded, turned back to the road. I wondered if I should have added the month and year.

Edie was waiting for us at the farmhouse. Savoury smells filled the air. The old mausoleum felt warm and inviting. When she heard Dan and the boys were coming over, Jean perked up, said the house looked lovely, and wasn't it fine to have such a welcome. By the time we got the luggage inside her energy had flagged. She was breathing heavily. When Ginny offered to take her up to her room, she said, It's full of boxes. I meant to go through that stuff last time I was home.

Lance assured her the room was ready.

My memories of that dinner are linked to dozens of photos and video footage shot by Frank. Voices and gestures, strangely disjointed. People having a good time but self-conscious in front of the camera, jittery, as though the ship we were on was heading into darkness, and we knew it and pretended not to care. Or maybe I only remember images that illustrate what I felt. There were no lulls in the party conversation. Everyone pitched in to keep it lively. Jean's homecoming is always a big event, but I couldn't help noticing the impact of Barry's presence. The masculine quotient soared. I recall an awful lot of handshaking as he made the rounds. Edie was palpably giddy, dispatching Lance to put the final touches on the meal while she showed Barry around the house and generally made him feel like a celebrity. They'd met at my various book launches. He came to the County a few times in the days when I was part of a local literary festival. But this was the first time a pillar of my Toronto life had actually penetrated the Cameron compound, and on an occasion that was strictly non-literary, although Edie pointed out that he had two clients sitting at the table. This, with Jean in residence upstairs, made it a royal occasion. At some point in the evening, she quietly convinced him to stay over in their guest room. He agreed but said he had to leave early the next morning to avoid rush hour. The celebration over, Ginny and I were left in the parlour with a half bottle of Pinot Noir.

I expected a full account of her mad dash to Rwanda, but all she wanted to talk about was the gala. I'd prepared a little speech about how significant it was to get that much recognition for a first novel, and winning a big prize wasn't necessarily the best thing for a long-term literary career. She cut me off in mid-flight: Wasn't the dress amazing?

Ravi had made a recording of the televised event and sent her a link. She'd watched it in their hotel in Amsterdam. *The Star* had published a photo of Barry and me sipping champagne, which she found online. You both looked fantastic, she said. Radiant, like totally established celebrities. I *love* that dress. Don't you?

Her face glowed. It struck me that the dress and accessories were Ginny's doing. I could not picture Barry Keehan walking into Holt Renfrew and buying such a garment. He doesn't even know my size. She'd had no intention of attending the Giller award, so pushed us forward and ran off to meet her mother.

I tried to turn the subject back to *Oyster*, but she said she didn't care about the prize. Writing isn't a contest. She said it was so awesome that Barry and I could be there to represent a novel that was partly, well, after all, mainly, my work. So it all worked out, right? How did the evening end? Did you go dancing till dawn?

So, Virginia as matchmaker, my mind reeled.

Lying in bed later, all I could think of was the looming problem of Jean's reaction, when she finally got around to reading the book. I had no energy for parsing Ginny's rambling about the social event of the century. The night we lost the Giller.

• • •

Jean slept for two days straight, taking brief bathroom and soup breaks. I wanted to call a doctor, but she wouldn't hear of it. On the third day, she got up at dawn, took a shower, drank a cup of coffee, and phoned the president of the local Catholic Women's League. The memorial service for Harold Cameron would take place, as scheduled ages ago, at St. Gregory's church. It soon became apparent the event was more than a tribute to the departed; it would also be a fundraiser for his favourite charity, the orphanage. She'd organized these events before, so there was an established procedure. With only two weeks to pull it off, we would all have to pitch in. Lance set up her laptop on the dining room table. She had a suitcase full of file folders, and in the space of a single morning, transformed the premises into an office hub. I listened from the kitchen as she barked orders on the phone, held committee meetings on Skype.

By suppertime she was exhausted, forced herself to eat a few tablespoons of mashed potato, and went straight up to bed. The next day, Father John dropped in to see how she was doing. He left with a fat to-do list.

Jean's transformation was bordering on miraculous. In less than a week, medicine, rest, and meaningful activity had rejuvenated her appearance and mood. The old Jean was back. Saturday morning over breakfast, I told her I had a few ideas about how the memorial might be shaped — at least the part about Harold. I would like to talk about how to honour him. She opened her agenda and booked me into a 1:00 p.m. slot. We met in her "office." She had a piece of paper in front of her with a long list of items, some waiting for check marks, and a notebook. The agenda for the big day was sketched out on a whiteboard tacked to the wall. There were no obvious gaps.

I said, I was thinking of adding something after the official event, say at five p.m., when we came back to the farm. I'd like to get Father John to bless a field, in Harold's honour. Kind of an onsite memorial to his many decades working the land.

She frowned. Where?

Near that big boulder, on the crest of the hill overlooking the vineyards. By the old apple tree.

A pause, during which her gaze drifted up to the ceiling. I don't see why not, she said. Although I don't know why you would want to do such a thing. I'm going to talk about farming in my eulogy.

I mumbled something about my intentions being different. She wrote two words in her notebook, which I could not decipher from my side of the table. We settled on 4:30 p.m., the day of the event. She warned me she might be exhausted by then and if so, would have to lie down.

I said I understood completely. No hard feelings. And since the plans seemed totally under control, I might as well catch the late train to Toronto. Of course I'll be back in time for the memorial.

21

The train pulling away from the station, ripping out nettles growing in my hair. I will never forget that moment, the image of my face reflected in the window with a familiar moving landscape as backdrop, though it had happened many times before. Settling into the seat, I held tight, forced myself to think forward thoughts, about my real life. City life. How many times have I lived this scene? The fun-house mirror of homesickness: can't wait to get there, then am glad to leave. This may be what the philosophers meant by eternal recurrence.

> What if some day or night a demon were to steal after you into your loneliest loneliness, and say to you, This life as you now live it and have lived it, you will have to live once more and innumerable times more; and there will be nothing new in it, but every pain and every joy and every thought and sigh and everything unutterably small or

> great in your life will have to return to you, all in the same succession and sequence....
>
> Would you not throw yourself down and gnash your teeth and curse the demon who spoke thus? Or have you once experienced a tremendous moment when you would have answered him: You are a god and never have I heard anything more divine.

Am I spouting lunacy to compare my tortured palpitations on a Saturday night in November to the great Nietzsche's lofty insight? By this point in a story that is, after all, a brief part of my long life, I don't know any other way to reconcile with the past than to remind myself that it all made sense, at the time. After Harold's death, I had no desire to understand or explain myself to the living. I was bent on tending to unfinished business on behalf of the dead, blinded by the mission to set my father free from the eternal recurrence of memory, to honour him as he chose to be honoured, in death. As I had not done in life. Make amends for having misunderstood and possibly ruined his old age by denying him connection to a woman who wanted to love him. How could I have been so selfish? I had wanted the centre of our family to hold after the loss of our mother. I expected Harold to sacrifice himself to the cause.

Returning to Toronto was an essential part of the plan. I had to pick up the ashes, which were waiting in a pewter urn purchased months ago, right after I convinced the management of St. James Cemetery that burying my father in a casket made of maple wood had been a mistake. I explained that in the panic following Harold's sudden death, we hadn't been aware of his last wishes as set down in his will. Now we were resolved to obey. I presented a typed letter, signed with four distinct signatures, different pens, because we had not been able to meet in person. I handed over a certified cheque to cover costs — and a Purolator account number. Please send the package to my home in Toronto.

I've learned this much about criminal activity: Once you embark upon a plan founded on a lie, subsequent lies pile up and if you are lucky, flow smoothly. Also, it is next to impossible to pull off a caper on this scale without accomplices. I had planned to rent a car, but Barry had heard about the memorial when he drove Ginny to the County. He was eager to witness the occasion. He had made quite an impression; I figured having him along might provide a buffer, should anyone try to resist. The Camerons are nothing if not well-behaved in front of strangers.

The urn was packaged in a cardboard box which just fit into a large suitcase on wheels. When we were on the highway, I gave Barry a shortened version of the plan, making an effort to sound casual. A family decision, I said. But please don't bring it up. Catholics tend to be queasy about cremation. He raised his eyebrows, reminded me he had been brought up Catholic too. I mumbled something like, There are many kinds of Catholic.

Edie and Ginny had tried to talk me into coming Saturday and staying overnight, but I didn't think I could stand the tension. I might not be able to keep from blurting out my secret. With Barry along, the risk of a leak increased. Whatever he thought about my plan to scatter Harold's ashes under the apple tree, he wasn't willing to say. I was fairly sure he'd figured out that no one else was in on it. I thought he'd appreciate being taken into my confidence, but he appeared nervous. Our conversation kept to small talk.

As we entered St. Gregory's, Lance was waiting, standing under a life-sized crucifix. Dan came over and instigated a round of handshakes. The church was full, mainly an older crowd, parishioners, and Dan's contacts. Jean and Ginny were already seated in the front row, beside the president of the Catholic Women's League and an altar girl whose job it was to help the guest of honour to the pulpit. The assembled rose as Father John and his servers trooped in from the vestry. He introduced Jean, prompting a round of applause as she joined him on the dais.

Jean's resurrection was complete and wildly impressive. She was dressed in a serious blue suit and wore a large crucifix around her neck, the standard garb of a modern religious order. She walked confidently, posture straight, head high. Her voice was strong and perfectly pitched for the amplifier. A commanding presence. She began by paying tribute to Harold for his generous contributions to the orphanage over the years, evoked his memory as an outstanding Christian, then turned to the situation in her Rwandan village, the hardships and successes, the dire conditions of lives we could barely imagine. She showed slides, an excerpt from the film, which she announced would open after Christmas at the Regent Theatre in Picton. Out of consideration for Jean's condition, Father John had turned the furnace up. It was stifling. I wanted to slip out of my coat but we were sitting shoulder to shoulder, so tightly packed it was difficult to move. I was weak with anxiety, and at one point sure I was going to faint. Other dignitaries came forward to thank her and urge the assembled to take out their cheque books. Afterward, we were invited to a reception prepared by League members, during which Jean sat at a table, taking donations. Meeting her people seemed to galvanize Jean's energy. She knew most of them, took the time to chat, shake hands, and recount details of the projects they were supporting.

As we were driving back to the farmhouse, Barry said, Well, what happens next? I looked over. He was smiling.

Do you know something I don't?

No, he said. Just that it is getting dark.

I'm prepared, I said.

When we reached the yard, Dan was standing at the kitchen door. He took me aside, said we'd have to postpone the site memorial until tomorrow. It's Jean, he said. She's fading fast. I went into the kitchen. She was sitting at the table drinking a cup of tea with Edie. I stood over her, said I hoped she wasn't going to renege on her promise to participate in this lap of Harold's memorial. After all, I'd driven all the way from Toronto for her fundraiser. She nodded, took a sip of tea. I could not read her expression, and for the first time in decades, I did not care what she thought.

The sun had already set. It was cold, but not bitterly so. A cloudless evening, full moon. For months, the scene had played out in my mind: late afternoon, a golden hour, it is snowing lightly. Or, apple trees are heavy with fruit, dusted with frost. Both would be great, but unlikely to happen together. This is a family ritual, backed by all. We form a solemn procession. Jean and Dan lead the way, Lance and Frank behind, carrying the brass container bearing the remains. Father John, Ginny, Glenn, Tommy, Edie, and finally me, last. And Barry. There is music. Not a requiem, please. A single flute or cello. Father John makes a few appropriate remarks, a reminder of the future upon us. Jean leads us in the Our Father. Lance and Frankie open the box. Just as the contents slide out, a gust of wind rises, sweeps Harold's ashes up and away. We stand in silent awe, watching his remains disappear over the fields, floating toward the lake, out of sight. The Cameron family is blessed with perpetual harmony and goodwill.

Reality was something else, although as time passes the two versions are beginning to merge in memory.

I'd lost my nerve, told no one of my plan, not even Father John. The boys had hockey practice. They were suited up and gone by the time we drove up the lane. I gathered the rest in the front hallway, and while Barry went out to get the box, revealed my plan, explaining succinctly why I had gone to the trouble of having Harold's body exhumed and cremated, without actually accusing anybody of disobeying his expressed orders. Dan blurted out a swear word. Lance laughed.

Ginny threw on her ski jacket and helped Jean into her coat. Edie walked beside Barry, who was towing the suitcase.

By the time we reached the rock, my heart was pounding. I looked over at Jean. Her face was grey. I half expected — hoped — she would take over, say a prayer, but her lips were stone. Dan kept his hands shoved in his pockets, eyes on the vineyard. I unzipped the suitcase, took out the box, opened the lid, and produced the urn. Barry stepped in and helped me lift it onto the boulder. Unsure of what to do next, and with nothing prepared, I began reciting the Lord's Prayer. *Our Father who art in heaven hallowed be thy name, Thy kingdom come, Thy will be done on earth as it is in heaven.*

I stopped. Could not remember the next line. Went back over the first line silently, hoping it would flow. Before I could finish, Edie (the convert) spoke up:

Give us this day our daily bread; and forgive us our trespasses as we forgive those who trespass against us; and lead us not into temptation, but deliver us from evil.

A chorus of *Amen.*

I slipped the latch and lifted the top off the urn, tipped it forward. The contents fell out, a heap of grey powder and bone chips, on the ground. A chasm of silence. We stood, paralyzed.

Dan muttered something about coming out the next day with a shovel and rake, then turned and headed back. The others followed. Barry helped me get the urn back in the box and the box in the suitcase. Not all of the ashes had spilled out. I had not thought about what to do with the urn after the scattering ceremony. Barry put it in his trunk, and we went into the house together. Dan produced a large bottle of whisky. Edie had assembled a tray of glasses. Dan poured doubles. Was it my imagination, or were they all struck dumb? None of them would look me in the eyes. Finally, I motioned to Dan to follow me into the parlour.

When we were out of sight, I said, I suppose you wonder what that was all about.

He shrugged.

Well, as Frank pointed out from the pulpit at Harold's funeral mass, he specifically asked to have his ashes scattered on the farm. Why did you overrule his specific wishes?

Shh. Keep your voice down. Look, Milly, you did what you did. Fine. Have it your way. But I, for one, think Dad should have spent eternity beside his wife, our mother, in a Catholic cemetery, in a plot they picked out together when they were both alive. Obviously. In case you didn't hear, the Pope frowns on the scattering of human remains.

I laughed out loud. Don't tell me you're quoting the Pope, I said.

Dan doesn't like to be laughed at. His voice rose, until I was sure the others could hear.

You know a man doesn't always get everything he wants in life. Even if he puts it in writing and makes vows in front of a priest. Life isn't fair, Milly.

He was obsessed with the problem of Edie. I was afraid he was going to cry. So I said, Fine, let's leave it at that.

But he wouldn't.

So from now on, every time I plough that field, I'll be turning over my father. Did you think about that?

On that note, I made my exit. We had left Toronto with the idea of staying all night somewhere, but my nerves were shattered. Jean took a coughing fit and had to be helped upstairs. In the commotion, Barry and I were able to slip out to the car. I was afraid he'd had too much whisky to drive, but he claimed he was stone sober. Nothing about his demeanour contradicted that judgment.

The trip back to Toronto was so unlike the journey there. I was high on relief. We talked about city things, the literary scene, the Snags, his mother's health, which was not good, meaning he had to do something about Tuscany. In no time at all, the Toronto skyline appeared, glowing, twinkling, inviting, and I thought, *God I love this place.* Especially the warm bed in the tiny house in the middle of a wild garden, all my own.

When we pulled up in front of the house, Barry got out and carried the urn inside. He left the car running.

You're welcome to stay the night, I said. Meaning, I hope you stay.

Without meeting my eyes, he said, Not this time. I'm bushed.

I tried to imagine a light-hearted comment that would make him change his mind. All I could think of was, *please stay*. Instead, I folded my arms and waited. His thoughts were somewhere else. He got back into the car and drove off.

22

Local doctors ascribed Jean's collapse to exhaustion, not a recurrence of malaria as we'd assumed. Of course I felt horribly responsible, making her stand in the November cold during a ceremony that could easily have been postponed until summer. I suggested she come to Toronto. She could stay at my house for whatever time it took to build up her strength. Surprisingly, she agreed. Ginny was thrilled, offered to sleep on the sofa and help out with the cooking. I'm guessing Jean figured it was a good idea to get away from Edie and her sound medical advice. My invitation was a tiny bit selfish. I kept imagining conversations we might have over tea in front of the gas fire. An endless litany of our voices carried on in my head, as I tried to see how we might reconnect, bridge some of the distance that had grown over the years.

The day we arrived in Toronto was warm and sunny. Jean was in high spirits, insisted on leaving the wheelchair behind and walked confidently up the sidewalk. I'm not an invalid, she proclaimed. It occurred to me she might be putting on an act, but she pulled it off. She ate a reasonable portion of whatever we put in front of her, and made a point of walking around the block, morning and afternoon. I heard her on the phone to someone at the orphanage. Proceeds from the fundraiser had surpassed expectations. My hunger for connection lingered but I could not find a way into the mound of questions on my mind, so kept silent, waiting for the moment. Jean up close is not the woman of my imagination. Or maybe I'm not myself when I'm with her.

Watching Jean and Ginny together, I could feel them tiptoeing around each other, avoiding subjects that might lead to disagreement. Ginny busied herself with making great meals and keeping the place neat and tidy, leaving little for me to do but observe. I was fine with that, grateful for her presence in what otherwise could have been a difficult situation. Hour by hour my desire to get to the bottom of things faded. I fell into that familiar Cameron state of being grateful just to see people getting along. A kind of paralysis, but you don't mind as the feeling takes over. Only later does it all seem so painfully false. And regrettable.

One night, out of the blue, at the end of an enjoyable dinner, Jean announced she was leaving for Boston the next morning. Another fundraiser was in the works. She must have made the calls from my room, where she slept, keeping the door closed. Ginny's face registered surprise, but she said nothing. She picked up the dessert plates and excused herself, saying she had plans to go out with friends. When we were alone, Jean surprised me by mentioning the book. *The World Is Your Oyster*, she blurted out, said it was a good title.

I laughed, a nervous reaction. So this was the moment. I asked her what she thought.

Well, it's not a comedy, Milly. Though I chuckled as I turned the pages, maybe for the wrong reasons. It's a fast read. Ginny tells me it's selling well.

It is, I said. And there may be a movie.

Wonder of wonders: I was so relieved to hear her speak calmly about the book. Until she said, Obviously, you had something to do with it. My daughter hasn't finished a homework assignment on time, ever. Your style is all over the place.

Jean, I had no idea the plot was based on Ginny's own story. I was mortified when she told me. I only meant to —

She laughed again, this time until her chest hurt.

Ginny's life story? I beg your pardon. Is that what she's putting around? Ha, that girl has a slippery grasp on truth. Or a wild imagination, however you want to define it. Yes, Ravi went through a period of sexual ambivalence — his personal crisis, if you will. It's not a unique experience. You lose someone you thought you knew. After a while, it all just becomes so, well, normal. What else? What about Ginny? She's been hell on wheels for years, since the day she started school. I'd have to say she seems to have calmed down since moving east. You're a good influence. The thing about the book …

She leaned ahead in her chair, glared at me: Don't you think it was a little cheeky to plagiarize yourself?

I had to ask what she meant.

That bit about me seeing Ravi and Ginny on TV and rushing down to the motel room to interfere. Isn't that the key scene out of *Erosion*? You — I mean the female character — are with that poet at a demonstration, his wife sees you both kissing under an umbrella and storms in to break it up? It's a good plot twist, but using it once is probably enough. Don't you think? Either she stole it, or you forgot. Is that possible?

A punch in the gut. She was right. I did not plagiarize myself, I followed Ginny's outline, but she had plagiarized me. How could I not have noticed? The truth is, once a novel is finished, you forget all about characters who've occupied your psyche for months, sometimes years. You have to wipe the slate clean to make room for a new bunch. I might have explained, but somehow a discussion of creative process did not seem appropriate. Even Jean at her kindest, most mellow, frail self still had the ability to sniff out my weakness and poke a finger.

You're right, I said. I made a mistake.

Lord, don't feel bad, she said. Does it matter? Will anyone notice?

I was stunned to observe how quickly Jean demolished a crisis I had dreaded for months: She was not at all bothered by seeing personal details in the novel; novels meant nothing to her. Troubled by imagined fear, I had destroyed *Oyster*'s chance for the Giller. (Jacques Durand later assured me it had been a contender before the jury was tipped off.) The crime she unearthed and joyfully ridiculed was self-plagiarism. So I was truly out of ideas.

While I struggled with this information, she turned to another theme: the Alford. She said she had high hopes for the business. I must have looked puzzled. My silence prompted her to explain that Lance and Edie are planning to open a restaurant and small hotel in the house, named after our soon-to-be-famous founding father, Alford Cameron. Haven't you heard?

I said something like, They've been talking about it for ages. I never paid much attention … busy with my work. Obviously, I had not succeeded in hiding shock.

Listen, Milly, she said. I'm sorry about Dad pumping all that money into the orphanage. I mean, I'm sorry for you. It's pretty obvious this house needs a lot of work. I'm sure you don't want anything to do with running a B&B in Prince Edward County. But I'm going to put a word in Dan's ear. He and Lance can darn well come up here and help you whip this place into shape. Did you say you need a new roof? I'm sure Dan's crew can take care of it. Don't let them off the hook. Don't be proud. This old house needs help. That's the least they can do, after indulging themselves with a vineyard and hotel on the family property.

My face burned, a dozen lashes on raw skin. Jean, speaking up about my lifetime of mismanaged finances? I had no doubt Lance and Dan would obey her commands. I was mortified. So this is what they think of me? A charity case, with no rights, only needs. Hours before my sister's departure from the continent, I had no desire to open what my brothers would call That Can of Worms. So I poured a glass of wine and kept my mouth shut.

To think I'd fantasized about bringing up the sad story of Veronica Lakey. That we might go back to that difficult time after Mom's death and figure out together how we could have made such a terrible mistake. I had so wanted to hear a version of events that explained our actions. Maybe the two of us could agree to share the burden of guilt. But raising the past was out of the question. I had floated around the house for a week, trying to make life as comfortable as possible for a woman who towered over me, both physically and emotionally. Now I was humbled, slumped in her shadow, with a whole new image of her to digest.

Morning came, her suitcases were packed. She sent Ginny to the corner store to fetch a certain kind of chocolate bar you can't get anywhere but Canada. I stayed busy washing a few dishes. Jean came into the kitchen. I dreaded the moment, buried my hands in the sink. She just stood there, staring out the window. Finally, I said, Jean, is there something you wanted to say?

We looked at each other. An awkward pause, then she put her hand on my shoulder and said, For goodness sake, Milly, lighten up. Live your own life, not just the lives of your made-up people. Lord, I don't know how you do it. Let alone why.

I was stunned. But just then Ginny appeared at the door. They scurried around assembling suitcases. Ginny had decided to accompany her to the airport in a cab.

She returned looking dejected, asked if it would be okay to stay around for a few days before going back to Montreal. I hugged her, assured her she would always be welcome in my home.

• • •

The week that followed was a time apart, my old life suspended. Ginny let down her guard, talked of her anxieties, dreams, recounted memories of our long ago past, the high and low points in between. The vast warmth and openness of this vital young woman filled every corner of my ramshackle existence, working like a salve on the oh-so-familiar wounds of dealing with Jean. Quite the contrast: Being around Ginny made me feel important and strong. Somehow what I said seemed to soothe her spirit. And I thought, *This is the essence of motherhood.* Nothing to fear, no worry. Just listen hard and respond in the same tone. Her whimsy and energy made my head spin. Her world seemed frightening and yet so full of promise. You can do anything you want, I heard myself say. A thing people say to young people, although life teaches otherwise. But in the presence of such vitality, and in the wake of Jean's departure from the continent, both our horizons seemed blissfully open. I was so grateful to have her around.

• • •

Sometime later, I got an email from Ravi. He'd decided to pay Ginny a visit in Montreal and would be spending a few days in Toronto on business. He wondered if we could have dinner. We went to a fancy restaurant attached to his five-star hotel. He was dressed in an elegant pantsuit that I could only describe as androgynous. A hint of eyeliner, silver bead earrings, a chic behind-the-ears haircut. He didn't look feminine so much as totally and originally himself. I settled in immediately, assured that our encounter would be comfortable. The consummate gentleperson, he'd read *Oyster* and thanked me for helping launch Ginny into the literary world, leading me to conclude that everybody knew some part of the story. The family scandal I had imagined and feared had been drowned out by the book's success.

Then, on the cusp of dessert, when I was least expecting complication, he launched into a new topic without preamble, obviously the point of his mission. He said he wanted to clear up a possible misunderstanding surrounding Jean's departure for Africa. For a while he had blamed himself, his decision to leave an old skin behind. I interrupted him, said I'd blamed myself for putting pressure on her. No, he said, Jean went to Africa for her own reasons. He pulled out a letter she'd sent him from Africa, and read it to me.

I didn't go to Africa the first time out of love for humanity, or to save the world. Not even because the man I married was wearing my jewellery! I went because I couldn't take the turmoil of dealing with an arrogant tall girl who spurned my affection, broke my heart. I dearly love our daughter. The day she was born I thought my life had reached perfection. I loved having a baby in my arms. Even as a toddler she was a darling. But as soon as she started turning into a little woman — that bathing suit Milly bought her! Not her fault. Or yours. She grew into a ball of ego. I hated being around her, the tantrums, demands, disrespect. I could feel her moving away from me, a fraction of an inch per day. Withdrawing her warmth. Turning me into the enemy. Everything I said she twisted around. I did not have the patience to endure adolescence. When I got to Africa and met the first group of skinny babies, their big hungry eyes, I knew that's where I belonged, in a world of needy children. Most people get worn down by the endless stream of suffering. Not me, I love every one of those sweet souls. I look forward to helping them, giving them good meals, watching

> them grow, learn to read and write. And
> leave. So be it! Bring on the next lot.

He put the letter back in his jacket pocket.

Well, I said, I didn't think Jean was capable of such brutal honesty. Especially when she's talking about herself. He laughed. He said the letter had come as a relief. He wanted to share it, because Jean is a big personality. She needs to be seen from all sides.

A hard core of family illusions dissolved with Jean's and Ravi's visits — Jean's revelations about the farm, my complete non-involvement, Ravi's evidence concerning her motives for leaving the family. I'd finally glimpsed the whole picture, the one that is on the front of the box containing a jigsaw puzzle but never exists in life, because there are inevitably missing pieces. When I struck out and created a public identity as Amelia Cameron, writer, I had willed myself onto the sidelines. My city persona was the self I lived. To the rest of the Camerons, I was Milly, off living elsewhere, appearing and disappearing according to her whims. Jean was right: My books were my life. My characters and their fate in the wide world of books were the centre of my existence. The great holiday times we'd shared were not part of our adult journeys. They were recreations of the past. We were close in the way only "happy families" can be close: by freezing time, being the people we were as children, when we lived with shared parents. We had never tried to bring our selves forward in time, until Dad died and we became orphans; then we had no choice but to step out of the idyll of childhood. Grow up. To do so inevitably meant growing apart, until we could someday come back together again as different people. Adults. Real people.

Ravi's visit brought all of this into relief. He had added a new layer of identity, assumed his true self. He was comfortable with the truth. He was someone to emulate.

A burden lifted. The weight of Jean. Whether I would ever see her alive again was uncertain, but the old Jean had disappeared for good. I had acquired a new version of who she was — as an adult. If only I could do the same for myself.

23

In the days that followed, I spiralled into sleeplessness. A string of nights when I would go to bed exhausted, much too early, wake up at midnight and roam the house, alternately frantic and bored, lie down and stare at the ceiling until dawn, then fall into a deep sleep, and wake up exhausted. I was on the verge of accepting this unfamiliar night shift as permanent when, in a pit of unconsciousness, the phone rang. It was 9:00 a.m. Delores. She wondered if I had tried to call the agency office. Seems their phones had been down most of the previous afternoon. She sounded nervous.

No, I had not called.

Well anyway, she said, would you be able to come in for a meeting? Today at 3:00 p.m.

I was so totally disoriented I said yes.

Standing under the shower, a burst of light. I decided it was time to formally sever my professional connection to Barry. No more hints he could ignore. Get a new agent, or live without one. My entire relationship to writing needed a deep, hard reassessment. I did not want to be part of a very old partnership while planning a new way forward.

What to wear posed a serious question. I decided on a feminine dress, off-white brocade with pearl buttons and a rolled collar, proper stockings, and shoes with heels. I did not want to appear as the slovenly bearer of bad news or, heaven forbid, a scheming businesswoman.

Barry was on the phone when I arrived. Delores sent him a text. He came right out, ushered me into the inner sanctum. We chatted amiably and quite falsely about the memorial (it was too soon to laugh). I thanked him for supporting me and taking the time to drive to the County and back. Think nothing of it, he said. Your family is always a pleasure.

I could have argued otherwise, but did not.

We sat down, Barry at his desk, me in the guest chair. He was not looking at the lake. The carpet under his feet was the big attraction as I outlined in clear, calm terms why it was necessary for us to end our professional relationship. I presented the argument calmly, being careful to allude to the high points of our years together, thanking him for the terrific effort he made on behalf of my writing. But the times were changing, etc., etc. This somewhat prepared speech went on longer than I had planned, mainly because he said nothing. He just nodded a few times, kept moving his gaze from my face to someplace behind my back, the painting, maybe. Finally, in an effort to wrap up, I said, We probably need to sign some paperwork, right?

He stood up, said, Yes, of course, I completely agree. Change is good. You mentioned it a while ago, I seem to remember. The night of the Giller. I would have followed up if I hadn't been so busy thinking of myself.

He pointed to a heavy antique armoire, salvaged from his old offices on Harbord Street, the only item in the room that was not designed by Italians or made of iron and glass. Completely out of place. I had always assumed it held sentimental value. As if reading my thoughts, he said he should probably get rid of it.

He walked over, opened the door. There was a small safe inside. He applied the code, the door swung open. From where I sat, the contents appeared to be mainly bundles of envelopes held together by string. He took out a bundle, waved it, and explained: These letters were written by my father to Mother over a period of thirty-five years. She was twenty when they got together. He was forty-five, at the peak of his powers as an English stage actor. Since he died his fame has slipped, although a lot of people in the business still revere his work. The thing is, after she had me, she couldn't keep up with him. I was a colicky baby. I balked at boarding school, refused to eat. So she had to stay back in London. She lived on his letters, long after he'd left her for someone else. In fact, she's still living on his legacy, and he's been dead for eons. Last summer, she was cleaning out the house in Tuscany and insisted I take these with me. Couldn't bring herself to toss them on the fire.

He paused, as if expecting a reaction. I thought, *Oh no, he's going to ask me to write a book about his mother.* I nodded, meaning, continue.

He put the bundle aside, reached into the back of the safe, and took out a small black velvet bag, brought it to the table, sat down, and slid it toward me. I froze. He opened the bag, pulled out a square box, flipped the lid, and handed it to me. Inside was a ring with a large green stone, apparently an emerald, surrounded by an exquisite circle of diamonds. An Italian surname was embossed on the satin lining of the box.

This belonged to your mother?

No, he said. I bought it in the late eighties, out of my cut of the movie rights to *Erosion*. I intended to give it to you, but the moment passed. You were so caught up in the whirlwind. Virtually unapproachable. I never found the right moment.

Looking closely, I saw there were actually two rings. The smaller, a simple band of diamonds, fit around the solitary emerald, until they looked like one. Obviously, a set. They were either antiques, or made to look old. The white gold setting was delicate, but sturdy. So beautiful.

This was all quite overwhelming. I was afraid to look at him, kept looking at the rings. From the corner of my eye, I caught a glimpse of him, arms folded.

I have a bit of news, he said. I've decided on a succession plan for this place. The business is changing so quickly, it only makes sense to bring on younger people. What the hell do I know about selling books in the twenty-first century? I'm not a bluffer. Well, ha ha, let's say I haven't kept up on trends in bluffing. Who cares? I'm starting with a six-month leave of absence. Buying a boat, sailing around the Caribbean. If that works out, I'll sell the firm.

Now I couldn't resist looking at him. My expression said, This must be a joke.

Silence, until he reached inside his jacket for his cellphone. I hadn't heard a sound, but he held his index finger up in the air, said he had to take the call. He mumbled a few words, nodded yes, yes, and hung up. Barely glancing at me, he said, Sorry, I have to go. What I wanted to say was, take this. In a sense, it's yours already. If things are going to change, I need to get some of this ancient stuff out of my possession.

At that, he left the room.

I had never been alone in Barry's office. The atmosphere was faintly creepy. He'd left the door to the safe gaping open. I figured if I touched anything, I'd leave fingerprints.

I sat there for what seemed like ages, soaking up the atmosphere. The office minus Barry reminded me of walking into the parlour after Harold died. He seemed more real, more present than he had ever been in life. This glamourous room, all for show, the bundles of old letters, an antique gift kept in a vault. A long-suffering gentleman poet, setting his past on fire. Colliding stories took my breath away.

Delores was engrossed in her computer screen when I entered her office. Seeing me, she jumped up, went over to the cloakroom, and took out my coat. My gloves dropped out of the sleeve. As she handed them to me, she looked at my hand and said, Amelia, those rings look marvellous on you. Such lovely slender fingers.

The glow of triumph on her face made it clear she thought a momentous occasion had just occurred. She was waiting for confirmation. But I had none to give. I was winded, as though I'd fallen into a bottomless well and was spinning head over heels. I started for the door.

When I looked back to say goodbye, she was standing dumbstruck, as if I'd just said, You go straight to hell. I was tempted to say, Sorry. But why?

How could I explain what I myself did not understand?

PART V

Spring

24

Milly, lighten up. Live your own life, not just the lives of your made-up people. Lord, I don't know how you do it. Let alone why.

The sting of Jean's final shot was tempered by the rush of departure. I made no response, but an image stays with me: her frail form disappearing into a taxi, the melancholy smile as she turned to wave, as if she didn't expect we'd see each other again. I jotted her words down in a notebook of musings kept for later consideration. A brittle dismissal of my life's work, but there is truth in what she said. Early success has been my cross to bear. I'm always judged against one accidental achievement. If there was a deeper literary culture in this country, maybe someone would have read the subsequent novels, noticed a plan developed over decades, at least ventured an opinion as to whether I've succeeded or failed. Or is this arrogance speaking? The misunderstood artist is a bore. Since those words came sliding out of Jean's mouth, I've had absolutely no desire to write. I've been living a life of action, walking around in her shoes so to speak.

On the positive side, she pretty well handed her beautiful daughter over to me. Beautiful, in the deepest sense of a great soul. Ginny is a big personality — energetic, generous, needy, funny, totally absorbing when she's in the middle of a dilemma or crisis, or is celebrating success, or just wondering, which is pretty well all of the time.

As the Giller hoopla faded, we talked through the experience at length and resolved not to let it interfere with our creative lives, or family ties. Barry urged her to capitalize on the notoriety and write a follow-up novel immediately. She was curled up on my sofa during one of her weekend getaways to Toronto when reflection took over. I'm not cut out to be a writer, she moaned. I don't have the concentration. You churned out *Road Trip* in no time, but that was after years of practice, right?

If there's one role I'm not prepared for, it's that of writing guru. There are no rules to be counted on, no such thing as a universal key to creativity, I said, then mumbled something about writing being bloody hard work, and you have to make it look easy.

I wonder if, these days, hard work even counts, she said. Maybe I need to get a few useful skills, like canning vegetables and carpentry. It isn't true that you can be whatever you want to be, is it? I'm thinking I'd like to do something useful.

This conversation lasted many months and probably contributed to my own lethargy on the writing front.

As the aunt of three newly grown-up nephews, I had only a faint idea of what young people were really like. Edie and

Dan's boys rarely shared more than a blast of their music or demonstrations of expensive toys. Ginny's stories of adolescence seemed tortured by comparison, although maybe because she talked about her life candidly, at length. Heartbreak, betrayal, body image turmoil, spells of anorexia, bouts of depression. I'd had no idea of how much pain a rogue notion of beauty could inflict on an otherwise balanced personality.

When Covid hit, she'd been working part-time in a restaurant, neglecting the unfinished M.A. Her flatmates moved out, she got laid off, couldn't afford the rent, and didn't want to live alone. I suggested she come to Toronto, bunk in with me until the virus passed. The move brought on a burst of energy, inspiring her to attack the mess and gloom of my badly neglected house. I agreed it needed a good cleaning, a bit of fresh paint. When you live alone, surroundings tend to fade from view. Her vision took a good four months to implement, during which time I was editing a stack of doctoral theses. Surrounded by chaos, take-out food boxes, and furniture covered in drop cloths, I sometimes went days without sitting down. Eventually, I fled to a local café to work.

Once the kitchen and bathroom looked like the magazine photos she had posted on the walls, she turned to the living room. I gave in, actually, gave up, began cleaning out my bedroom closet.

While hospitals overflowed with seriously ill people, the world caught up in a pandemic that showed no evidence of subsiding, I could not summon the will to resist Ginny's assault on my environment. Her health regime included regular exercise. I agreed to keep her company. Ten thousand steps a day. Seriously? At first, I did it out of concern for her well-being. After a few weeks, walking turned into routine. I lost weight, gained energy, hardly felt like myself. My old life with space for reverie was a diminishing mirage.

Where it all was leading, I could not imagine. But the turning point came suddenly, during the weekend Dan came to the city. At Ginny's request, he arrived with a tool box, camera, and tape measure, prepared to give my house a roof-to-basement inspection and draw up a comprehensive reno plan, which she had convinced him to mastermind and supervise. By the end, I would have a valuable piece of city property. I was furious but stayed silent, promised to think it over. We ate in a fancy restaurant. Dan paid.

As soon as he left the next morning, I purchased a For Sale sign at Home Depot and stuck it outside the house. A blizzard of real estate agents descended, each one suggesting a more ludicrous list price than the last. I signed with the one who was least obnoxious and sent the others away. Ginny embarked on the mission of finding a quiet, two-bedroom condo, with no further potential. I could not yet foresee myself living alone, with the mental space necessary to start another book, but I had not lost hope.

Every move I made in those days was overshadowed by a feeling that we were entering a new phase of history. A time when it would be necessary to remember that all civilizations rise and fall. Eventually, the planet will burn itself out, which will be an event quite distinct from the reality of individual mortality, although there were many reminders of that too. Friends and relatives died, relationships were destroyed by arguments over who was to blame for the death toll, how the virus could have been brought to heel without shutting down an entire economy. As soon as pandemic panic subsided, other catastrophes took over. An anxious atmosphere settled in on everyday life, and it has yet to lift.

25

In the midst of Ginny's grand reno adventure, Lance's life went into a tailspin.

Trudy and her boys disappeared. Overnight, her house was empty. Rent paid to the end of the month, they were gone. He was devastated, angry, frantic with worry. I visited him for a week, spent many hours listening to him relive their time together. The more he talked, the more I became convinced that there was more to Trudy's story than we'd been told. Lance kept throwing out juicy hints but would not be questioned on details. I went back to Toronto feeling I'd done him no good at all. The nurturing gene is not easily coaxed to life.

One night Dan got a call from the Picton hospital. Lance had arrived by ambulance. A bartender in town had found him in the parking lot, unconscious, after a severe beating. I rushed back to the County and was there when he came out of the operating room. He was too groggy to speak, but in the days that followed, police provided enough clues to fuel a serious questioning of the victim.

Trudy's husband had not simply been "out of the picture" as Lance had described him. He was doing time at Kingston Penitentiary for armed robbery. Trudy and the boys had moved to the County from out west so they could be close enough to visit him until he got out. The missing husband had somehow found out about Trudy's relationship with Lance, and in a fit of rage ratted on several accomplices in return for early release. As a result, he and the family were sent into the witness relocation program, with new identities and a far-off address. It was friends of the accomplices who had roughed up Lance, acting under the assumption that he knew of their whereabouts, which he did not.

Dan was furious, also deeply concerned about our brother's well-being. Lance was released after a few days in the hospital, where he miraculously escaped getting Covid. He stayed with Dan and Edie for two weeks, then moved in with friends in Picton. We heard nothing for months. I was distracted by the chore of purging a life's belongings and keeping up with Ginny.

When Lance did reappear in our lives, it was via a phone call from Toronto police, saying he was in bad shape and could we come right away. The Lance we met was hardly recognizable. He had lost a lot of weight and was clearly in the throes of a relapse into old demons he'd struggled with in Vancouver. This was not the kind of struggle I could manage by offering him pots of tea and a chance to talk, or following him on long walks. He needed serious professional rehab treatment. We were now fully aware and could not pretend otherwise that a member of our family would be walking on the edge for the rest of his life.

In such a situation, you ask yourself how this could possibly have happened. The boy Lance was a sunny blond, blessed with our affection. Maybe he was spoiled. Maybe he felt neglected by his parents. Or, it might have been the company he kept out west, the culinary scene. Such was our innocence that we believed every curse had its logical cause. There must be a reason for this weakness in our kin. Dan blamed Trudy. It came out that Lance had known from the beginning about Trudy's husband's jail time. Something in the dramatic situation must have suited Lance's personality. Over the years, he had brought home a series of amazing women but never took the big next step. We never knew why. Fear of commitment? That's hardly an explanation, more like an observable trait, but what did it mean? If he were a character in a novel, the author would have to provide an explanation. But real life is a bottomless mystery. No certainty is reliable.

I was sorry I hadn't spent more time with Trudy. She was the last person who got to know Harold before his death. She must have insights into what he'd been thinking, feeling, in the weeks before he died. I still hope someday she will pop up in our lives and talk about the missing piece of our father's life. Lance hopes so too. Surely their story isn't over.

When Lance got back on his feet, it was thanks largely to the challenge of transforming the old farmhouse into a smashing hospitality hub. The Alford, a boutique B&B and fine dining emporium. After his troubles, we all fully supported the project, knowing it was probably our brother's best chance of a stable, fulfilling life.

Edie had enrolled in a private culinary program that took her to Toronto for a week or two at a time, on regular intervals. Some of her classes went online during the pandemic, but the occasional personal appearance was expected. There was talk of her renting a studio apartment, but once lockdowns settled in, she decided not to bother, instead, bunked in with friends she'd met in the program. Meanwhile, she and Lance both worked hard to meet their deadline for a spring opening.

My old room was named the "Amelia Cameron Suite," with the walk-in closet turned into an ensuite bathroom, swanky new light fixtures and furniture, refurbished plaster painted soft greys and cream, and of course, books: a trophy case, which I was invited to stock with my novels and select favourite titles.

Mother's oval mirror is a main feature of the new decor. The first time I saw myself reflected under contemporary lights, I was shocked by how much I look like her, around the eyes especially, a skeptical look that can't easily be turned off. The left eyebrow is a question mark over anything else the face may seek to express. Exercise and healthy eating have put a glow in my complexion, enhanced by Ginny's choice of makeup — so simple, even I can make it a routine (her words).

Thanks to an eighty-dollar haircut, I can pass for a successful, together human being. Ginny chose the coiffeur and booked me into bi-monthly appointments, so there is little chance of falling off that wagon.

Wandering through the Alford for the first time, I felt a gush of gratitude. The reno project had given Lance a reason to stay on his feet. Our late parents, our shared childhood, seemed far away, part of the buried past. We were now thoroughly adult, responsible for the fragility of others, which was all around us. All around me. Dan, Edie, and I saw a lot of each other during the turmoil of Ginny's breakout and Lance's breakdown, with enough to talk about that we never needed to face our personal struggles. In an earlier time, I might have confided in Edie that Barry was leaving his agency, leaving Toronto to become a carefree sailor in a perpetually warm climate. By talking about him, I would have given her permission to ask how I felt about his leaving. I would have told her, then I would have known. As it was, I put my head down and dealt with each day as it came along. That's what happens when the centre of a family goes into eclipse. Certain patterns and connections disappear. For months, I rarely had occasion to see or speak to Barry, except for minor issues around *Abstraction*, which came out during the pandemic and sold surprisingly well. The idea of dropping him as my agent became a moot point; I wasn't writing anything, I hardly needed an agent to hold my hand.

One morning, I opened a large piece of mail from his office and found two copies of the *London Review of Books*, latest edition, with my name on the cover. A terse note from Barry: *thought you'd be interested.* Inside was a five-thousand-word essay by an accomplished literary critic — both a famous novelist and member of Oxford's English department — about my work. I sat down and immediately read it through. She noted the success of *Erosion*, pointed out thematic ties to what followed, but mostly she focused on the later novels, a thorough and respectful synthesis. What she found was not exactly what I'd thought I had written, but interesting nonetheless. It was deeply gratifying to see my life's work out in public, on its own terms. I imagine this is what a parent feels when her grown child makes good in the world. Oddly, I was hit by a sense of loss, the nest is empty.

26

Out of the blue, Edie called to suggest a dinner with the younger generation in Toronto, where her boys were ensconced at various learning institutions and CV-enhancing menial jobs. It was just after the house had been sold, before Ginny and I moved into the new condo. My belongings were in storage, I was staying with a friend in the suburbs. Ginny was on a trip with Ravi. Edie said she'd get us a hotel room so I wouldn't have to face an hour commute after dinner at the fancy restaurant she'd booked.

It was a wonderful evening, even though the two of us felt like periphery characters rather than the presiding matriarchal hosts we'd imagined. Toward the end of the meal, she leaned over and whispered in my ear, Don't order dessert, we'll go somewhere else.

Great idea, I thought. It was clear this party could carry on without us; she was leaving a credit card.

As we left the restaurant, she hailed a cab and directed the driver to a tiny Italian bistro in a residential area of town. Crazy place for a restaurant, I remember thinking. It was well after 10:00 p.m. Won't they be closing soon? She'd made a reservation. There were only ten tables, two of them occupied by diners near the end of their meals. We took a corner table for two. She advised me to order the tiramisu, the house specialty. A few minutes later, a distinguished-looking Italian gentleman appeared from the kitchen bearing two plates of dessert. Edie introduced him as Marco, the chef and owner. He asked if he could join us. Of course, we said yes.

Edie and I sat opposite each other, Marco at Edie's side. He was her mentor and teacher. He actually ran the cooking school out of his own restaurant. He had worked in various top establishments in Italy and Paris before relocating to Toronto. After my life over there fell apart, he added. They exchanged brief glances. I had a sinking feeling this detail was relevant.

The rest of the conversation is misty. As I recall, he raved about Edie's talents in the kitchen. A natural, he said. She's so full of creativity, ready to try anything. He had a lot to say about Edie. It took my breath away to realize he was talking about every part of being with her — cooking was only one element. This was not a scene I wished to witness. It was a struggle to swallow one bite of the legendary dessert.

At one point, Marco reached his little finger out and wrapped it around hers. Edie's face was already glistening pink. She shivered. I had forgotten what it was like to be in the presence of raw eroticism. The fire. I could hardly look at Edie. I thought back to our weekend at St. Anne's when she'd said Dan had nothing to worry about. What had she meant? Was that before Marco? Was she looking for someone, but hadn't found him yet? Now I was being introduced to a strange man with whom she clearly had a past, to say nothing of the obvious present, and surely, some kind of future.

I said I was tired and got up to go. Edie walked me to the door, leaving her purse at the table. I won't forget the picture of her standing on the street corner. Early November, mild after a cold snap, it was snowing lightly. She leaned against a street lamp pole, as if she had no will to move.

Amelia, I'm sorry, she said. I really thought this would blow over. But it didn't.

My mouth was dry. I nodded, tried to smile.

She looked up at the sky and sighed. The thing is, she said, I just don't know what to tell Dan. I mean … Do you suppose he knows? I feel so bad. He gave up his chance to be mayor, hoping I would run. I tried, honestly. I gave it a lot of thought. But in the end, I'm just not that outgoing. It's a shame he missed the nomination date. Thing is, I really dread facing him, after all that. I still care about him, a lot. We'll always be in each other's life, but this thing just happened. Well, I was wondering if you could, you know, break the ice?

I found the turn of phrase odd, to say the least. Isn't breaking the ice something you do to get a party started? If ice breaks on a lake, you fall through and die quickly. That's what telling Dan would mean. I said I'd think about it and let her know.

I guess you aren't coming back to the hotel?

She shrugged, said, I should.

Never mind, I said. I can manage. Say good night to Marco for me.

I stumbled out of range of the restaurant before letting out a forceful howl that may or may not have included sound. Walked for ages before finding a cab. Barely remembered the name of the hotel. The driver had to circle around until a building looked familiar. I could say how cruel she was to leave me alone with this information, but recalling the sight of her body held up by the lamppost, the halo of anguish around her swoon state, I could think only of how powerless she looked in the snowy moonlight. Recollection of the moment may be clouded by my ancient theory that you have to give up everything before getting that kind of love. A coward's calculation, to be sure. Maybe I was simply jealous that she had beautiful Marco waiting for her embrace, and I had the empty single bed in a hotel room for two. I figured I would get up in the morning and know what to do. Until then, it was a matter of feeling bad, and putting in the hours before dawn.

• • •

The next day was Sunday. I phoned Barry, and after a weak attempt at small talk, asked if he might have time to drive me to the County.

I'm planning to stay with Dan for a few days, I said. He'll be happy to see you. Sorry for the short notice. Only if it's convenient.

He sounded surprised to hear from me but recovered quickly, claimed he'd actually been thinking about getting out of the city. Should be fun. He could pick me up after lunch.

Although Barry occupied almost no space in my life at that time, he and Dan had become pals around the Alford project. Barry had a slew of well-heeled friends in the County and was enthusiastic about the prospects of an upscale B&B with a stellar restaurant in a new version of the old homestead. He'd been networking his Toronto contacts about the evolving venture. Dan and Lance welcomed his input. Dan swore the hospitality business made a lot more sense than being mayor of bloody Prince Edward County. Barry said it was a pleasant break from the book game, which he was planning to leave as soon as he found a buyer for the agency and finalized purchase of a boat.

It was mid-afternoon by the time we got on the road. I had regained balance and was able to fill the air with amiable conversation. I said nothing about the real reason for my sudden desire to visit Dan until we reached the County. Then I said I had something to talk over with him. Could we go somewhere for a coffee? His expression turned grim. He asked me where I wanted to go. I said it didn't matter, we could just pull over to the side of the road. He shook his head, barrelled ahead into

Wellington and his favourite bistro, the Drake. When we were ensconced at a table with a stellar view of the lake, he relaxed, said he was feeling peckish, why didn't we order a few snacks.

Go ahead, I said. I'm not hungry. The fact is, Dan and Edie are splitting up.

Oh shit, he said. I thought it was something terrible. Like you'd had bad medical news. Have you?

No.

You're sure, no tests?

No symptoms. Barry, listen. Edie's met someone. She's leaving Dan for an Italian. It's a disaster.

Yes and no, he said. His favourite pat answer, meaning nothing.

The waiter arrived, took an order for coffee. For the longest while, neither of us spoke. I cried quietly, wished I'd never had the foolish idea of bolting to the County, when my heart was breaking.

After a long pause, he said, Look, it's not as though we haven't had signs. She's never here. Haven't you noticed? She's been talking about getting a studio in Toronto for ages. I mean, hello. Is that a marriage?

Dan will be absolutely devastated.

Dan will survive, he said. Trust me.

This was not the consoling wisdom I expected from a lifelong friend who had dried my tears on so many occasions.

This event marks the end of our family, I stammered. Lives will be ruined.

Whose life?

Well, Dan's. And mine.

Dan can manage his life. Besides, he probably knows.

You think so? Did he say anything to you?

Not directly. He's not a confider. But I've noticed lately he has an eye for female sparkle. Waitresses, passersby.

Oh, well then, it's all sorted out! Edie can be replaced by a barmaid from the nearest beer hall.

That wasn't what I meant. Yes, it's terrible when a long-standing couple decides to separate, but —

Dan didn't decide anything! This is something that happened to him!

Well, there's nothing anybody can do about it.

So you're siding with Edie? How predictable.

I was almost shouting, which is not done at the Drake. Or for that matter, anywhere in Ontario outside the downtown Toronto core.

He reached for my hand, then stopped, pulled back, sat up straight.

I know you're feeling bad. And I understand why. Dan and Edie were the heart and soul of Clan Cameron. They have been since your mother died. All families need a centre, or they cease to exist. That centre is part of your world view, your creativity. Your amazing energy. As the man said, things fall apart, the centre does not hold.

Yeats. "The Second Coming."

Indeed.

Our coffees had arrived, been sipped at, and were cold. It was late afternoon, almost dark. I said, We should be going.

Does Dan know you're here?

No. But he's pretty well always home.

A few hours ago, the idea of telling Dan about Edie in person had seemed necessary, urgent. Now I was deeply not in the mood. We walked to Barry's car. My head was aching, I could hardly stand. When we were sitting inside and buckled up, I said I don't want to go to Dan's. Guess you should take me back to Toronto.

Are you sure that's a good idea?

Probably not.

Well, what should we do?

I said, let's go to Picton. Have another coffee and decide.

He started the car.

• • •

The Royal Hotel is a magnificent phoenix sitting in the middle of dear old Picton. The hub of the town in the late 1800s, the hotel had fallen into ruin a century later and was rescued at the last minute by people with an eye for grandeur. I had never been there before, and felt like I'd stepped through the looking glass into somewhere exotic. The main floor is all creamy marble and pale wood, every sculpted detail a product of fine design. Barry was perfectly at home, a touch smug, as though he had been putting up with a lot from Picton and finally felt comfortable in an ambiance meeting his standards. We took a table an the bar near the window, my back to the street, Barry looking out on passersby. He ordered a double scotch. I decided to sip at a martini and collect my thoughts.

I asked about his boat. Had he bought it yet? He said the owner had changed his mind about selling. But he was on the lookout for another.

I'm surprised you decided to sell the agency, I said. The Snags seemed to launch you in a whole new direction. You seemed so enthusiastic.

Do you mind if we don't talk business?

Not at all.

He ordered a refill, and I thought, *You won't be able to manage the 401 if you keep that up.* He seemed to read my mind, took a generous sip.

I said, I think we should probably stay here tonight. I'm going to ask about rooms.

Relax, he said. It's off-season. There won't be a problem.

I suppose not.

There was this huge balloon of silence hanging in the air between us. I wasn't sure why my mind was numb. I had no idea what he was thinking, if he was thinking. Barry's a master at making conversation, so when he chooses not to, you feel hung out to dry. I'm no good at small talk, I need to be drawn out.

It struck me that words had to be important, or not be used. So I said, I'd rather you didn't leave the agency just now when I'm, well, in transition.

He leaned forward, as if to confide. But said nothing.

Sorry, I said. You don't want to talk business. I won't.

You can talk about your writing, he said. Just not about the agency. Are you saying you have a new idea for a book?

Not really, no. Quite the opposite. It's my life that's stalled, or in transition. Writing will follow, probably. See, I don't know how to go on when the ground under my feet keeps shifting. Too much change, I don't know who I am anymore. Or what to do.

Well, that is a dilemma, he said.

Were you really going to run away to sea and leave me agentless?

When the time comes, I'll find you somebody.

If I ever write again.

You will. I'm sure of that, he said.

That's the problem. I know you're sure. Even when I'm not. How will I manage?

What do you mean?

How will I manage without you?

For the longest time, he said nothing, his face set in a faint quizzical expression. Then he waved at the waiter, asked for an espresso and the bill. I'd hardly touched my glass and took a sip to remind him.

Why don't we see if they have rooms here? I said. It's off-season. The place feels empty.

I'm perfectly capable of driving, he said. If you've changed your mind, I can give Dan a call. Drop you off.

No. Don't do that.

You're in a strange mood, he said. What is it?

Everything. The rings. Why did you give them to me, after such a long time?

I was cleaning out the office, in preparation for leaving.

That hardly answers my question.

You would have rejected them on any other occasion if I had not simultaneously declared I was leaving town. Dear Amelia, can we at least be honest, once? The only way out of this thing is for one of us to jump off the ledge. So I volunteer.

Silence.

You're right, I said. You did a brave thing.

Trouble is, I haven't actually done it yet. Left. I'm still sitting here with you. Hoping. Opening myself for more obfuscation. Rejection. Whatever. Oh shit, this is so pathetic. I don't even mean it. Look, Amelia, I am truly ready for a new life. I got to keep a wad of money from my mother's house. The plan is to spend it and then blow my brains out while drunk on champagne. Unless something else comes up in the land of two-piece bathing suits, which it very often does. What's wrong with that plan?

Nothing. But it will leave me broken-hearted by the knowledge that I lost the best relationship of my entire petty life without giving it a chance. Sorry to make this about me, but I have always had you in my writing life, up close, helpful, dependable, kind, and it is only these past few months as stand-in mother of a famous young novelist, caretaker of a reformed drug addict, and shoulder-to-cry-on for an abandoned husband that I've had the opportunity to realize how much you mean to me. You know, it's one thing to fall in love. It hits you. There's a sound, a rush of adrenalin. But to wake up in love is to feel vaguely dizzy, like you might have had a dream, or not. So you carry on. There's no pressing need to analyze or chart the feeling. It just is, like water or air, neither of which one can live without. But who goes around saying, Wow, air! Amazing. Waiter, bring me a glass of your best water. If scarcity is what it took to make me see how bonded we are, fine. But I am not going to apologize for not making that dramatic leap years ago. I was busy, trying to write. Ugh! So selfish. I'm sorry we never tried. That's all. I'm out on a limb, Barry.

What do you want from me, Amelia?

I'm asking you to consider us in your future career deliberations. I mean, personal too. Personally. You and me. Us.

Long pause. His eyes drifted to the street outside. He stroked his chin.

Well, that is a highly original proposal, he said. I shall have to think about it.

Sleep on it?

That too.

We could stay here, I said. If they have rooms.

• • •

Barry insisted on taking a suite called the Royal Gala, and slapped his credit card down without letting me see the price. It was more like a luxury apartment than a hotel room, with a gas fireplace, white bathrobes, all the trimmings. We ordered dinner in and stayed up all night, talking, running through certain scenes from the past in the soft light of a new mood of openness. For a man of action, Barry had given a great deal of thought to incidents and conversations I had either forgotten or relegated to a notebook under the heading of things to be reconsidered at a future date. The atmosphere was warm, somehow thrilling, two people walking on tiptoes. We stayed a second night, by which time the endless conversation felt like a voyage leading somewhere, though in circles. He said we should stay in cruise mode until we settled our fate, and if there wasn't going to be a future together, then we should part as friends and never speak of this time again. I had flashes of Jane Austen penning his dialogue. Yet keeping in mind the effort he'd gone to, forging those rings, keeping them for decades, I could hardly say he was speaking out of character.

On the issue of telling Dan about Edie, he categorically refused. Families need boundaries, he said. He could never in a million years open such a conversation with a grown man. He advised me to drop it too. I was surprised how deeply relieved this command made me feel. He's right, of course. There never could have been such a conversation between Dan and me that ended well.

By the morning of day three, it seemed this conversation would never end. We would just have to move it to another location. Human beings are, after all, nesting animals.

27

Barry took it upon himself to tell Dan our news, which reportedly cheered him up. What my brother said was, Huh. Well, nobody can say you two are rushing into anything.

Neither of us wanted a big public party, with the inevitable head-table remarks dripping in sarcasm. So we opted for a mid-week appearance at city hall, Edie and Dan as witnesses, thereby confirming that whatever their personal status they will always be part of our family. Ginny was flower-person, because she would never have forgiven being left out.

In place of celebration, we decided to pool resources and build a house together. Barry found a spectacular waterfront lot, far enough away from the Alford so that we wouldn't be bothered by the roar of success. He and his architect pal designed the plans, a modern Tuscan villa, with a great kitchen and adjoining dining room big enough for a table seating twelve, ready to receive Cameron family Sunday dinners and holiday celebrations. Dan offered his services as general contractor, mumbling something about making a contribution to my new life. We never did discuss his appropriation of the farm, but guilt is a powerful force; I'm more than happy to take my inheritance in labour. He's over here almost every day with his crews in the various trades.

This will be a beautiful home, when finished. For now it's not much more than a building site with a camping kitchen, two offices, and a bed. We moved in anyway at the first sign of spring. The only completed room is my top-floor workspace, which has windows on four sides and a large writing table facing the lake. The vista is mesmerizing. I can sit here for hours, watching the snow melt, the birds returning to the fields, lost in reverie. Blessedly few books are on display; mainly they're stacked boxes, along with notes on my unfinished doctoral thesis on Milton, various drafts of novels, scraps of research — evidence of a life I hardly remember. It's shocking how a change of environment can transform a person's sense of self. If I open one of my novels at random, the characters seem like strangers. I would have to start at the beginning, and can't bring myself to do so, for fear of disappointment.

I am supposedly writing another novel. Anita Brooks is waiting, my editor from the glory days of *Erosion*. The problem is, I don't seem to have a novel in me. I'm up here in the clouds, talking to myself, pretending to do what I've always done. Maybe I'm haunted by Jean's remark that I wasted my life on *made-up people.* As if she's the poster girl for paying attention to the here and now. I wonder if she'd recognize herself in the pages of "fiction"?

The only story that feels worth telling is the story of what happened after Harold's death. How he became my personal saint, the talisman waved against my faults: selfishness, self-absorption, neglect of kin. My failure to love and live out emotion and help other people love and connect. Harold Wicklow Cameron, I am so sorry I participated in the campaign to keep you from loving Veronica Lakey and enjoying her love in your old age. For my penance, I vow to remember you with immense love and respect for the rest of my life, and in your name to honour, above all, the blessing of love in all its glorious, mysterious forms.

Savoury smells are drifting up the staircase. Barry will be making dinner. I'll go down now. He'll ask how my day went. I'll say very well, thank you. And yours? He'll bring me up to date on the latest news from the hagglers' market of literature, then apologize for complaining. I will take the glass of wine he offers and tell him, don't worry, my darling, it doesn't matter.

THE END

Acknowledgements

This book has been ages in the making. Among the many writers and readers who have contributed helpful comments, I would like to mention Sharon Baltman, Ann Walmsley, Janice McAlpine, Carlyn Moulton, Anna van Valkenburg, Hilary McMahon, Leah McLaren, and John Goddard. To those I've unwittingly left out, a huge thanks as well. Every reader counts! A special thanks to Robyn So, my editor at Dundurn, who bravely redefined the meaning of finished and sent me back to the keyboard. *Oyster* has benefitted immensely from your close engagement. The Dundurn team are my dream team, from publisher Meghan Macdonald, who fished the manuscript out of the submissions pile and gave me a call, to everyone in production and publicity, including Elena Radic, Laura Boyle, Eden Boudreau, and their various assistants — a seemingly bottomless anthill of talented people at Dundurn working on getting *Oyster* to readers.

About the Author

Photo by Michael Mcleod

Marianne Ackerman is the author of three novels (*Jump*, *Piers' Desire*, *Matters of Hart*), two collections of short stories (*Holy Fools + 2 Stories*, *Mankind and Other Stories of Women*), and dozens of plays, including *L'Affaire Tartuffe, or the Garrison Officers Rehearse Molière*, *Woman by a Window*, *Céleste*, *Venus of Dublin*, *Triplex Nervosa*, *Rooftop Eden*, *Famously*, *Departure Plans*, and *The Night Before Lear*. She was co-founder and artistic director of Montreal's Theatre 1774, as well as founding editor of *The Rover*, an online arts magazine. Born in Prince Edward County, she spends winters in Montreal and summers in a century-old stone house in Prince Edward County.